Curse of Texas Gold

Curse of Texas Gold

Bradford Scott

WHEELER
CHIVERS

This Large Print edition is published by Wheeler Publishing, Waterville, Maine, USA and by BBC Audiobooks Ltd, Bath, England.

Wheeler Publishing, a part of Gale, Cengage Learning.

The text of this Large Print edition is unabridged.
Other aspects of the book may vary from the original edition.
Set in 16 pt. Plantin.
Printed on permanent paper.

LIBRARY OF CONGRESS CATALOGING-IN-PUBLICATION DATA

Scott, Bradford, 1893–1975.
Curse of Texas gold / by Bradford Scott.
p. cm. — (Wheeler Publishing large print western)
ISBN-13: 978-1-59722-692-9 (pbk. : alk. paper)
ISBN-10: 1-59722-692-0 (pbk. : alk. paper)
1. Large type books. I. Title.
PS3537.C9265C87 2008
813'.54—dc22 2007044816

BRITISH LIBRARY CATALOGUING-IN-PUBLICATION DATA AVAILABLE

Published in 2008 in the U.S. by arrangement with Golden West Literary Agency.
Published in 2008 in the U.K. by arrangement with Golden West Literary Agency.
U.K. Hardcover: 978 1 405 64414 3 (Chivers Large Print)
U.K. Softcover: 978 1 405 64415 0 (Camden Large Print)

Printed in the United States of America
1 2 3 4 5 6 7 12 11 10 09 08

Curse of Texas Gold

Chapter One

Like a torpid snake, the Mojo Trail slithers through the Puerta Hills. It slips stealthily past the juncture of the Old Spanish Trail and the famous Chihuahua Trail, slides furtively into Boraco, the railroad town, and flows onward toward the distant Guadalupes. On the eastern edge of the Guadalupes it becomes the main street of Sotol. Then it winds past ill-omened Jericho Valley, enters the remote fastnesses of the Guadalupes and steals across the state line into New Mexico.

The Pueblos used to pad over it, long before the Spaniards brought the horse to the New World and thereby greatly extended the Indian's scope of activity and increased his capacity for devilishness.

But the Mojo was old long before the Pueblos first used it in their treks from south of the Rio Grande to their cliff dwellings in what is now New Mexico; and even then it had a sinister history, being the natural route from one wasteland to another — the wastelands always provide sanctuary for men who make sinister history.

Fifty miles northwest of Boraco, the Mojo begins its weary climb over the towering backbone of the Puertas. With a bristling cliff on one side and a sheer drop into a shadowy canyon on the other, it winds steeply upward, with many an almost right-angle turn where the cliff wall thrusts out at the traveler and the dark gulf to the south reaches hungrily for horse and rider. The trail is narrow here, with barely passing room for two teams taking it slow and easy and exercising the utmost care.

Up this steep and winding gradient, rode a man mounted on a magnificent black horse, full eighteen hands high, whose glorious mane was like to a ripple of dark flame. The rider was worthy of the splendid animal he bestrode. He was over six feet in height, broad of shoulder, deep of chest, narrow of waist and hip. His pushed-back "J.B." revealed crisp black hair and a broad forehead singularly white in contrast to his deeply-bronzed cheeks. His nose was prominent and his rather wide, good-humored mouth, grin-quirked at the corners, somewhat offset the tinge of fierceness evinced in that hawk nose, the jutting chin and the lean, muscle-rippling jaw. From the bronzed countenance, under heavy black brows, gay, reckless gray eyes looked out upon the world and found it good.

Thus, with a song on his lips and laughter in his eyes, Ranger Walt Slade, named by the Mexican *peons* of the Rio Grande river villages El Halcon — The Hawk — rode the Mojo Trail, headed for Sotol, thirty miles distant.

Slade looked forward to his mission Sotol and predicted he would find it an interesting town. There had been six killings and as many robberies in and around Sotol in the past two months, with some cattle stealing thrown in for good measure. This was why an angry Captain Jim McNelty had dispatched his lieutenant and ace-man to the section in answer to a plaintive bleat for help from the local authorities.

"Some sidewinder, or maybe two or three, raising the devil and shoving a chunk under a corner over there," said Captain Jim. "See what you can make of it, Walt. Got a letter from the sheriff yowling about conditions. Name's Clem Baxter and he sounds to be all right. Get in touch with him and the chances are he can give you the lowdown. Just the usual deviltry that takes place in all gold strike sections, I reckon. Figure you shouldn't have too much trouble getting things under control. Those old cowtown sheriffs get panicky when something comes along to bust up their routine. Most of 'em are cowhands that got elected to office and following a cow's tail most of their lives don't do much to develop intelligence. Honest and dumb, that's what you usually find 'em. Quick on the trigger and slow in the think tank. Be seeing you."

Walt Slade wore the efficient, unconventional garb of the rangeland with careless grace. About his lean waist were double cartridge belts and from the carefully worked and oiled cut-out holsters protruded the plain wooden handles of heavy black guns. His Ranger badge, the famous silver star set on a silver circle, was not in evidence at the moment but tucked away in a cunningly concealed secret pocket in his broad leather belt. He preferred not to reveal his Ranger connections for the time being, having found that it was sometimes to his advantage not to do so until necessary.

His habit of working under cover had built up a peculiarly mixed and not altogether enviable reputation. Plenty of people knew him to be a Ranger and admired and respected him — "the ablest and most fearless Ranger of them all." Which was saying considerable. Some who did not know him as the ace-man of the most illustrious commander the famed Border Battalion ever had, were wont to say that if El Halcon wasn't an owlhoot he missed being one by the skin of his teeth. Slade did nothing to discourage this erroneous conclusion, although he well knew it made him fair game for any ambitious gunman out to get a reputation, having found out by experience that a man of dubious standing could ofttimes gather valuable information, the sources of which would be closed to a recognized peace officer.

As Shadow climbed the long and winding slant of the Mojo Trail, Slade talked to him jovially in the fashion of men who ride much alone. The big black seemed to understand, for he wheezed and snorted, nodded his head wisely at times and at others shook it vigorously in emphatic disagreement. Slade chuckled and began humming a song as he lounged gracefully at ease in his comfortable Mexican saddle.

Suddenly, however, he straightened, his bearing became alert. Some of the sunniness left his gray eyes and there was a tightening of his lean jaw. He leaned forward in an attitude of listening.

From somewhere ahead, thin with distance, had sounded the hard, metallic crack of a rifle shot, another, and another, evenly spaced, purposeful.

Slade listened intently for a further repetition of the sounds, which did not come. Quite likely some trapper or hunter shooting at a varmint, he decided, and was about to resume his comfortable, loose-jointed slouch when he heard a faint rumbling, an almost inaudible mutter that steadily increased in volume.

The concentration furrow between El Halcon's black brows deepened, and he tightened his grip on Shadow's bridle. There was something ominous to that steadily loudening rumble that hinted at wheels spinning altogether too swiftly for safety on the hazardous track. He pulled the black to a halt and sat rigid in the hull, his head again bent forward in an attitude of listening, his gaze fixed on the trail a hundred yards ahead, where it vanished in a bristle of growth which took advantage of a sudden widening of the crumbling ledge on which the track ran.

"Shadow," he muttered, "that sounds like a — Blazes! It *is* a runaway!"

From out the dark tangle of pinon and chaparral crashed a wagon drawn by four frantic horses. Despite the mad speed with which they raced down the trail, the heavy wagon kept jamming the trees against the hind quarters of the wheelers, driving them insane with fright. They in turn lunged against the leaders, squealing and biting and infecting them with their panic. The driver of the wagon sagged against the high back of his seat, lurching and lolling, his head rolling on his shoulders, the reins limp in his nerveless hands.

In a single swift glance Walt Slade took in the situation, and with the same swiftness he acted. He wheeled the black on bunched hoofs, leaned low in the saddle; his voice rang out, "Trail, Shadow, trail!"

Like the released coil of a spring, the great horse shot down the trail, his irons drumming a low thunder on the flinty surface. And after him raged and roared the hurtling death and destruction.

Under ordinary circumstances, the wagon horses would have been no match for Shadow, but now, driven insane by terror, they raced down the steep track with the speed of madness. They were on the black's very heels before he got into his full stride and for hundreds of yards he did not gain a foot. Indeed, the crashing rumble of the runaway seemed louder in Slade's ears as he glimpsed, not far ahead, an almost right-angle turn which to take Shadow must slacken his breakneck speed or court destruction. It was well nigh impossible for him to take that turn at the speed he was traveling.

Slade's mouth tightened as he visualized what would happen did the racing horse stumble or fall. Instinctively he glanced over the crumbling lip of the trail and into the shadowy depths of the canyon which flanked it, down through five-hundred feet of nothingness to where swift water glinted and black fangs of stone reached hungrily upward.

And even in the tenseness of the moment his attention was momentarily distracted from his own appalling situation. Down there in the depths he was certain he had detected movement, a flickering of shadows among the shadows, that appeared to be horsemen riding parallel to the grim race with death half a thousand feet above.

Perhaps they had spotted the runaway and were racing to be present when the inevitable happened. Slade jerked his eyes back to the trail and gave his whole attention to negotiating the perilous turn that raced toward him with frightening speed.

A flickering glance over his shoulder

estimated the space between him and the hurtling team, another the distance to the turn ahead. It was going to be close, horribly close. His hand tightened on the bridle. He put forth his strength steadily, surely, careful not to break the rhythm of Shadow's stride. With a slow, steady pull he turned the black's head to the right. Shadow snorted, curved his glossy neck, leaned toward the threatening bulge of the cliff; let him hit the jut of stone and he would rebound into the canyon. He knew it and his rider knew it, but Slade also knew he must crowd the cliff to the last possible inch if he were to take the turn.

Slipping and skating, Shadow rounded the bend. Once he was all but off his feet and his skidding irons showered fragments of stone over the lip of the ledge, but Slade's steely strength steadied and held him. Behind him crashed the runaway, the breath of the lead horses hot on his flanks. Their squeals of terror shrilled in his ears. With a desperate lunge he whisked around the bulge and scudded down the straight-away like the glint of a sunbeam on a wave crest. Behind him sounded awful screams of terror and despair.

There was a rending crash as the wagon caromed off the bulge, a screech of sliding metal and an awful grinding sound. Slade, twisting in his saddle as he fought to master his frantic mount, saw the tangled mass of horses and wagon shoot over the lip as if hurled by a mighty hand. The dead or unconscious driver was flung from the seat as a stone from a sling. Arms and legs revolving wildly, he plummeted downward.

"God Almighty!" Slade gasped.

From the slowly overturning wagon, two more bodies had catapulted like pips squeezed from an orange. Down they plunged, after them a rain of what looked like sacks of grain, with the spinning wagon and the still plunging horses following.

The awful screams of the doomed horses thinned to an agonized wail. Up from the dark depths geysered a far-off thudding crash, followed by silence utter and complete.

CHAPTER TWO

Cold sweat breaking out on his face, Slade finally pulled Shadow to a skittering halt. With another effort he turned the gasping horse and rode back up the trail. He reached the bulge, rounded it and pulled up on the very lip of the cliff edge. Leaning far out over the awesome chasm, he peered down. His lips formed a startled oath.

Sprawled among the dark fangs of stone he could see the splintered wagon and the crushed horses. Several men were running toward the pitiful debris. He spotted a clump of saddled horses a little distance up the canyon from where the wreckage lay. He leaned over the lip, peering with interested eyes at the activity on the canyon floor. Then with blurring suddenness he flung backward, dragging Shadow's head up with all his strength.

On his hind legs, the snorting black surged back from the edge. And even as he did so, something screeched through the air and fanned Slade's cheek with its lethal breath. From the canyon depths drifted the crack of a gun.

With Shadow hugging the inner cliff wall, Slade dismounted. He slid his heavy Winchester from where it snugged in the saddle boot and crouched low, glaring angrily at the cliff edge. For a moment he crouched motionless, then with infinite caution he crept toward the lip of the ledge. He was out of sight from the men below and should they fan out into the canyon he would see them as quickly as they could sight him. Cocked rifle at the ready, he waited.

With a smashing crack, a bullet slammed the cliff face scant feet above his head. He ducked instinctively as flying rock fragments showered him with stinging splinters.

Where the devil did that one come from? It could not have come from below and hit the cliff at that angle. It had to come from somewhere above. Slade's head flung up as he felt the wind of the next one. This time he heard the rifle crack, following the arrival of the slug with an appreciable space between. His gaze flickered across the canyon, searching the ragged crest of the cliff that formed its far wall, where objects stood out hard and clear in the flood of morning sunshine. He hurled himself sideways and down as he caught a gleam of shifting metal.

"That one hit right where I was, but now I got a line on you!" he growled apropos of the distant rifleman.

He clamped the butt of the Winchester against his shoulder, his eyes glanced along the sights. A spiral of smoke wisped from the black muzzle.

Slade saw the puff of dust where the bullet struck a foot or two below the man crouching on the cliff top, barely visible against a straggle of growth, his position revealed by the tell-tale glint of sunlight on his rifle barrel.

Up came the Winchester muzzle, the barest fraction of an inch. Again Slade's eyes glanced along the sights. He squeezed the trigger just as smoke puffed from the barrel of the distant rifle.

As he fired, Slade writhed sideways, shifting position as much as he could. Even so, the slug ripped the shoulder of his shirt and grained the skin beneath. The drygulching hellion could shoot!

But heedless of the burn of the passing lead, Slade raised himself and stared across the canyon as the distant gunman, looking little bigger than a doll, pitched over the cliff edge and, turning slowly in the air, plunged to the rocks a thousand feet below.

Slade instantly inched forward a few feet and shifted his gaze to the canyon floor. No one was in sight. His mind worked swiftly.

"Stay put, feller," he flung over his shoulder at Shadow and began crawling around the cliff bulge, hugging the rough stone, his eyes never leaving the west half of the canyon floor, which was all that his restricted range of vision included.

But as he rounded the bulge, just as he had surmised, his range of vision broadened, due to the lessening angle as the trail turned more to the east. He stood erect, the rifle clamped against his shoulder.

Three men were riding away from the wreckage of the wagon, headed up canyon. Slade's fingers tightened on the trigger. Hard upon the report came a distant yell of pain and anger. Slade saw the rearmost horseman reel in his saddle. He clutched the pommel for support and kept his seat. His companions twisted in their hulls, flung rifles to their shoulders. Bullets stormed about Slade, smacking against the cliff face, kicking up puffs of dust from the trail, but he was in the shadow while those below were outlined by the full glare of the sunlight. Rock-steady, his own barrel lined with the target below. Again he saw a man leap sharply in his saddle and knew he had scored another hit. But before he could line sights a third time, the group sent their horses charging around a bulge of the canyon wall and were out of sight.

"Guess that will even up for peppering me with hunks of rock!" El Halcon growled as he lowered the smoking Winchester. "Don't know what this is all about, but gents who throw lead take the chance of getting some thrown back."

For long minutes Slade stood with his gaze fixed on the bulge, but the dark edge discovered nothing of movement. Evidently the horsemen had kept going, with two of their members winged but not seriously.

"What the devil is this all about?" Slade wondered aloud.

Neither Shadow nor a querulous crow circling about overhead was able to answer the question. Slade glanced at the sun, then into the shadowy gorge which grew less shadowy as the sun climbed the long slant of the eastern sky. Coming to a decision, he mounted Shadow and rode swiftly down the trail. He had to back-track almost five miles before he could enter the canyon. The semblance of a trail snake-slithered among the rocks and straggles of growth. Slade followed its tortuous course and finally reached the wrecked wagon.

The vehicle was smashed to splinters, the horses to pulp. All around, the ground was littered with beans, flour and grain spilled from the burst sacks. To all appearances the wagon had been packing provisions, probably to some outlying ranch. But Slade suspected it had also packed something else decidedly more valuable.

The bodies of the unfortunate occupants of the wagon were battered almost beyond human resemblance, but not battered enough to obliterate the bullet holes puncturing the chest of each. Slade was of the opinion that they were dead when they went over the cliff, which under the circumstances was a merciful blessing. Gazing at the horribly disfigured faces, he strove to reconstruct the tragedy.

The rifleman who had tried to kill him had ridden along the rimrock cresting the far wall of the canyon, from where he had a clear view of the trail. With three accurately placed shots he had killed the wagon's occupants. The driver had not yet set the brakes before dipping down the steeper grade. The wagon rolled against the wheelers and set them running, which was very likely what the drygulcher figured they would do and had held his fire till just the right instant. Meanwhile the group in the canyon had ridden for the hairpin turn which they knew the uncontrolled equipage would never take. The drygulcher riding the rimrock had spotted him, Slade, at about the same time the bunch in the canyon did and had cut loose on him with his rifle. Fortunately, opposite the bulge the canyon widened considerably and his aim wasn't quite good enough.

The important question, to Slade's mind, was why had the bunch wanted to send the wagon off the cliff, which they indubitably planned to do? Seeking the answer, he went over the canyon floor with the greatest care, following a widening circle with the wreckage its center. After some minutes of searching he unearthed a smashed rifle and an equally smashed sawed-off shotgun. The picture was beginning to clear up.

All three dead men were armed with sixguns that had remained in their holsters despite the fall. The additional weapons indicated that the wagon had been manned by a driver and two guards. Undoubtedly it had packed something of value, probably a gold shipment from Sotol consigned to Boraco, the railroad town.

Slade turned out the dead men's pockets

in hope of finding some clue as to what the wagon had carried, but he discovered nothing of value. Replacing the various articles, he mounted Shadow and rode across the canyon, splashing through a small stream that ran down its center, and approached the west wall. Here he dismounted and after more searching located the body of the drygulcher. It was not pretty to look at after its nearly a thousand-foot tumble.

The man's face was too badly marred to retain any significant features or expression. All Slade was able to learn was that he was short and slightly built. There was nothing about his nondescript range costume to set the wearer apart from other riders of the prairie or wastelands. Nor did his pockets show anything of significance.

But the man's hands interested Slade. By some singular chance they had been neither broken nor badly bruised by the terrible fall. They were smooth, well-kept, the nails delicately pointed. Slade could not be absolutely sure, but he was of the opinion that the fingertips had been rubbed with very fine sandpaper.

Those hands bespoke a card dealer. The nails carefully pointed to leave an almost impreceptible mark on the back of a card, the sandpapered fingertips sensitive enough to detect the marking as the cards were shuffled and dealt. Yes, beyond dispute, in life the man had been a crooked dealer or gambler. That he also had been a crack shot with a rifle was just as undeniable, as Slade was unpleasantly aware.

He would have liked very much to get a look at the horse the drygulcher rode, but getting to the rimrock of the west wall was impossible from where he stood, and very likely the cliffs continued to be unclimbable until the hills miles ahead, where the canyon evidently ended, were reached. He dismissed the notion as impractical.

It would be equally impractical to try and follow the horsemen who had fled the canyon. They would be familiar with whatever ways led through the hills and he was not. Even if he were able to trail them, he could not hope to reach them before dark when everything would be in their favor. Also, as the canyon appeared to run almost due north, it was reasonable to believe that they were headed for Sotol, where perhaps he would run into them again, under more favorable circumstances. He mounted Shadow and rode back to the wagon.

He did ride up the canyon a short distance and with satisfaction noted an occasional blood spot on the stones. Anyhow, the hellions had something by which to remember him. But the spots were not frequent enough to indicate that the two punctured gents had suffered serious injury. With a last glance at the grisly scene of snake-blooded murder, he rode back down the canyon, regained the Mojo Trail and resumed his interrupted journey to Sotol, the sleepy cowtown that almost overnight had undergone one of those startling metamorphoses peculiar to the Southwest.

CHAPTER THREE

From where the Chihuahua Trail crossed the old Spanish Trail, northwest to the eastern fringe of the Guadalupe Mountains, is a region that has never been — and doubtless never will be — disturbed by the plough. It is a land of canyon and mesa, of desert and chimney rock. Here the prevailing vegetation is greasewood, coarse chino grass, sotol and other yucca, white and yellow mescal and thorny brush.

Here, too, however, are great reaches of splendid grazing land where the tall grasses of the prairie region grow, needle and wheat grasses, the coarse bunch grass the Panhandle calls buffalo grass and the curly mesquite rich in the distilled spirit of the blazing Texas sun and the sweet rain of the dry country.

It is a land of the deer, the javelina, the panther and the bear. It is a land, too, of men, many of whom have gathered unto themselves the attributes of the fierce, wild, treacherous but courageous creatures with whom they share the danger and the beauty, the loneliness and the grandeur of the desolate wastes which are their home.

It is a land of legends and stories, of lost mines, of fabulous "mother lodes", of hidden treasure grimly guarded by bones of murdered men. It is the home of the vicious little sidewinder, the pygmy rattlesnake of the desert that strikes without warning, lashing out in the blurry sideways motion from which it gets its name. The home, too, of the giant rattler of the mountains, its cheeks fat with venom that drips like brown ink from its curved fangs. Here is seen the vingaroon, a large whip scorpion that smells like old vinegar when alarmed and which is popularly supposed to be exceedingly venomous, but isn't. The evil looking little hellion is often the prey of the Gila Monster whose bite really is as poisonous as its orange and black "wampum" coat is beautiful.

Among the eastern spurs of the Guadalupes, tradition places the legendary Sierra de Cenizas — Ashes Mountains — from where the Spaniards under Captain de Gavilan took loads of nuggets and "wire" gold. But de Gavilan and his men perished in the great Pueblo uprising of 1680 and the secret of their golden hoard died with them, or so tradition says.

These jagged eastern spurs of the Guadalupes send out long granite claws, running down into the lowlands and dividing them into deep and rugged stretches of valley where sometimes white water foams against the black rocks.

This is cattle country and always will be. And because it is cattle country, the cowtown of Sotol drowsed sleepily in the late spring sunshine as a horseman fogged it down the trail that wound like a gray ribbon into the northwest.

Sotol wasn't much of a town. It wouldn't have been there at all if it weren't for the spreads to the north and east. The spread owners and their cowboys had to have some place where they could enjoy themselves and Sotol was the result.

The permanent residents of Sotol built dobes, cabins and false-fronts. Gentlemen with business instincts housed general stores, saloons and gambling halls behind the false fronts. By some process, never definitely understood, Sotol became the county seat of a county which was about the size of an average eastern state and had a population which would compare favorably with that of a well-settled city block.

There were a number of interesting things about Sotol, but the town's proudest boast was the Dun Cow saloon, which squatted among the dobes and cabins and false-fronts like a fat and amiable sow in the midst of a litter of many piglets.

Old Sam Yelverton, with more money than he could possibly spend for whiskey, conceived, planned and began building the Dun Cow when he was drunk. When he sobered up, pride — and the necessity of upholding the fable that he, Sam, never got drunk — obliged him to finish the darn thing. When it was finished, the Dun Cow was high, wide and not handsome. Cowboys rode a hundred miles out of their way to view the huge-beamed and ceilinged room, the hanging lamps and the mirror-blazing back bar. The Dun Cow was something to see and talk about!

But the crowning glory of the Dun Cow was neither lamps, beams nor mirrors. While on his extended spree, which took him as far east as the capital, old Sam had viewed and admired a set of French windows. Nothing would do for Sam but those windows, but French windows necessitated a building in which to place them. The Dun Cow was the result.

Anything more incongruous and out of place than those tall, hinged windows extending from floor to ceiling would be hard to imagine. Many-paned French windows don't go well with warped board sidewalks and lanterns hung on poles to serve as street lights.

Those windows greatly intrigued old Ben Sutler. He would sit forking his rangy skewbald and stare at them, shaking his white head and rumbling in his awesomely deep bass voice. Ben was a desert rat who had been prospecting for gold for more than half a century, and not finding it. He was nearing seventy and he and the black-and-white horse had been part of the scenery around Sotol for so long that nobody could recall the town without them.

The skewbald was Ben Sutler's joy and pride. It had fire in its eye and the devil in its heart. It was a killer to everybody else, but in Ben's hands it was as gentle as a lamb is supposed to be. It would do anything Ben told it to do, go anywhere he told it to go.

Ben Sutler had a way with all critters. Squirrels would eat out of his hands, coyotes crouch within the circle of his campfire light, Gila Monsters crawl around him without swelling up like pizened pups. Beansoup Perkins once told an awed audience in the Dun Cow, "And there was that old hellion settin' on a rock with a dadblamed rattlesnake big 'round as my leg creepin' up his arm. Snake reared up and looked Ben Sutler square in the eye and, gents, I've always heard tell that a snake can't smile — but, gents, that snake was smilin', or I'm a sheepherder!"

Beansoup Perkins was a person whose statements were not generally believed, but folks who had seen hummingbirds take crumbs from between Ben Sutler's bearded lips were inclined to feel that for once Beansoup had made a mistake and told the truth.

Sotol drowsed sleepily in the early spring sunshine, and the skalleyhootin' horseman hit the main street with a crash and a clatter and a yell like a panther with his tail caught in a crack. Up the street he bulged, white hair and white whiskers fanning it in the wind. Directly ahead was the Dun Cow, the panes of the French windows glinting in the sunlight.

Opposite the Dun Cow, the rarin' skewbald made a fishhook turn. Old Ben Sutler howled like a Comanche with a new scalp that didn't fit his own head. The skewbald answered with a ten-pig squeal — and old Ben sent him straight for the nearest pair of

French windows.

There was a crash like a fair-sized mountain turning over onto a crockery store. The French windows went to blazes in a regular blizzard storm of smashed glass and splintered frames. Old Ben and the skewbald never stopped for so much as a splinter or a toothpick. The skewbald's irons chugged on the hardwood floor, skittered, clawed. Clean across the room he skated, bringing up smack against the bar, snorting and foaming.

"Whoo-o-o-pee!" remarked old Ben, and mountain lions two miles back in the Guadalupes slunk for cover.

Old Sam Yelverton spouted out of the back room like a boiling over coffee-pot. "You spavin-hocked blankety-blank-blank!" he yelled. "You can't bring that horse in here!"

"The heck I can't," howled old Ben. "He's here, ain't he?"

"You mangy pelican! You're crazy as popcorn on a hot stove!" screeched Sam. "Get him out of here! Look at my window!"

"To blazes with your window! I'll buy you all the windows 'tween here and Heaven! Give me whiskey!"

"You couldn't buy the foam off a glass of beer!" bawled Yelverton. "You ain't seen a dollar for so long you forgot what an eagle looks like! Somebody hand me a shotgun!"

But old Ben let out another whoop, hauled a big buckskin sack from his saddle pouch, whirled it around his head and dumped it on the bar. A second later and you could have heard a pine needle drop on the roof of the Dun Cow.

The whole end of the bar was covered with big nuggets and hunks of "wire" gold!

There's something about raw gold that sets men's pulses to pounding. Men who are unmoved by a handful of minted double-eagles will grow deliriously excited over an equal amount of nuggets or dust. Here is something primal, elemental, the treasure of the dark places of the earth, born of fire and the travail and the awful shudderings of terrestrial upheavals. The molten yellow blood of the young world now frozen by the cold breath of years, ages and eons beyond number.

The bartender goggled at the pile. He choked, gurgled and finally broke the silence. "G-good gosh! Ben, where'd you get it?" he squeaked.

"Whiskey!" roared Mr. Sutler, uncompromisingly.

The barkeep scooped up a bottle, and his hand shook. Old Ben grabbed the bottle, knocked off the neck, clean as a diamond-cut, with his hand, and poured half of its contents down his throat.

"Whoo-o-pee!" he said again, and the hanging lamps jumped and jingled.

The barkeep scooped another quart. "Have another drink, old-timer, have two drinks!" he invited. "Belly up, gents, have one on the house!"

There was a concerted rush for the bar. Old Sam Yelverton voiced a thin wail of protest, but nobody heard or heeded him. They crowded around Sutler, sloshing glasses held high.

"Here's to good old Ben!" they whooped. "Have one on me, Ben! Have another one!"

Old Ben gulped a swig from his bottle. His white beard wagged, opened in a grin of pleased content. His filmy little blue eyes gleamed and watered.

"Friends!" he opined. "All friends! Ev'body my friends!" He took another drink, looked mysterious, beamed on everybody present. "Going to let you all in on secret," he declared. "Going to tell you where I got gold!"

The crowd drew closer, eyes flickering from the heap of nuggets on the bar to old Ben's face.

"The sun shines bright on my ol' Kaintucky home!" boomed Mr. Sutler, beating time with his nearly empty bottle. The crowd gave a hollow groan. Mr. Sutler smiled happily. "Gents, you'd never guess!" he chortled. "No, sir, you'd never guess!"

"We ain't good at guessing, Ben," somebody pleaded.

"Reckon that's right," Mr. Sutler agreed unexpectedly. "Ain't going to make my friends guess, nohow. Gents, I got this gold out of the darndest hole in the Guadalupes. She come from Jericho Valley!"

There was a stunned silence. "But, Ben!" somebody protested at length, "there ain't nothing in Jericho Valley but snakes and arsenic springs and falling rocks. Ain't safe to even walk through there."

"She come out of Jericho Valley," old Ben reiterated stubbornly. "That's where I got her. And there's plenty more — more'n plenty more. Enough for the whole town, and then some. Rec'lect them shale banks down underneath the cliffs? Well, them shale banks are as thick with gold as a John Chinaman pudding is with raisins. That's where I got her, gents. Help yourselves!"

The bartender suddenly shucked off his apron and tossed it under the bar. He went over the bar in one jump.

"Gents," he bawled as he went through

the swinging doors so fast the paint smoked, "gents, I'm resigning! Help yourselves!"

A wild yell greeted this announcement — and the stampede was on!

It was a humdinger. Old Ben Sutler didn't exaggerate when he declared the shale banks in Jericho Valley were as thick with nuggets and "wires" as a cow cook's pudding with raisins. Getting it out was hard and dangerous work, but the claims men staked were unbelievably rich.

In consequence, things happened to Sotol. The sleepy cowtown, drowsing in the sun, awoke with a screech and a yowl. Its population doubled, tripled, quadrupled and kept growing. New buildings went up so fast a gent who had been plumb at home on Sunday night got lost in the same section on Tuesday morning.

Old Sam Yelverton, to his utter dismay, found himself the owner of the most prosperous business in the county. He had to hire new bartenders, many of them, more dance-floor girls, waiters and dealers. In despair he hired a head dealer to look after the games and keep order. The head dealer, Crane Arnold by name, was a lean, sinewy individual with an affable manner, a pleasant word for everybody, whether the individual had a hundred dollars to spend or only a dollar, and a genius for stopping trouble before it really got started. He could be hard, if necessary, and his mild blue eyes could turn flinty when the occasion warranted. But he seemed to prefer to be quiet and courteous and friendly at all times. He got himself a reputation and the admiration of old Sam his first night in town by easily outplaying Yelverton and several of his cronies at stud poker — which was no light thing for any man to do. That's why Sam hired him.

Under Crane Arnold's hand, the games were absolutely straight. A man was safe in the Dun Cow no matter how much gold he had on him or how drunk he got, more than could be said for some other of the town's places of entertainment. Arnold's reputation as a square-shooter grew and business in the Dun Cow got better and better. Sam Yelverton, who couldn't begin to spend what he already had, found himself making more money hand over fist, and collecting added worries and responsibilities with every dollar that plunked into his tills. Finally, in despair and disgust, he sold out to Crane Arnold, on long time payments. Henceforth, happy and satisfied, Sam Yelverton drank and played poker in the Dun Cow as of old, and had nothing to worry about.

Crane Arnold also appeared to have nothing to worry about. The Dun Cow continued to prosper and Arnold had no trouble meeting his notes when they fell due. His face habitually wore an expression of peace and content.

But there wasn't much peace in Sotol and its environs, and there were plenty who were not contented. There were killings in the streets of Sotol and killings, some of them mysterious, in arid, heat-scorched Jericho Valley. Fights and killings, however, were to be expected in a gold-rush town. What gave the reputable business men and the sheriff more concern were holdups and killings along the formerly little-traveled Mojo Trail. The Mojo was the shortest route, and the one always open, no matter what the season or the weather, to Boraco, the railroad town. Before the gold discovery, only shipping herds and supply wagons used the Mojo frequently. Now things were different. The supply wagons, many more of them, freighting wares to take care of the greatly increased demand for merchandise, still rumbled down the mountainside, and the trail herds still used it. But in addition there was the transportation of precious metal from Sotol and all too often the metal never reached its destination. Gentlemen with no respect for property rights took care of that, often in a daring and ingenious manner.

All sorts of schemes were tried to thwart the robbers, but all too frequently the robbers saw through the strategems and set them at naught. The businessmen, gold shippers and other honest citizens howled to the unresponsive Heavens and showered maledictions on the hapless head of Sheriff Clem Baxter who added to his force of deputies, to no avail.

And in the course of the weeks and months, Sotol developed another less sinister and more intriguing mystery — the mystery of Ben Sutler's gold.

Old Ben staked no claims, nor was he ever seen to toil under the ever-present menace of the overhanging cliffs and slopes that towered over the shale banks. But Ben continued to bring in gold. None of the Jericho Valley claims, rich though they were, ever produced such nuggets and "wires" as old Ben poured upon the bar of the Dun Cow. When asked where he got them he'd chuckle creakily and twinkle his filmy blue eyes. For days at a time he would loaf about town drinking and gambling and giving away money. Then one night he would vanish. Weeks might pass, or only days, and he would reappear, always with a plump poke.

Men tried to trail Sutler to his hidden mine, but the old prospector was wily and nobody knew the hills as he did. While the baffled searchers were still combing the brakes and canyons Ben would reappear with his creaky chuckle and his filled poke.

And then Ben Sutler disappeared and did not return. Days grew to weeks, to months. There was a chill of early autumn in the air at night and the season was fast approaching when mining in Jericho Valley would be impossible.

A howl, louder and more indignant than even those of the harrassed gold shippers, went up. Men felt they had been defrauded. Something had happened to Ben Sutler, and with it something had happened to the secret of Ben Sutler's gold. A fresh storm of wrath descended on the grizzled head of Sheriff Clem Baxter. In desperation the sheriff wrote an urgent letter to Captain Jim McNelty, imploring Rangers to police the section and clean out the owlhoots.

And then, some days later, Sheriff Baxter learned something. Just what he learned nobody ever knew for sure. For Clem Baxter was a secretive man and did not see fit to take anybody into his confidence. He merely told Clifton Yates, his newly-appointed chief deputy, that he was taking a ride and would see him later. Alone, the sturdy old peace officer rode to sinister Jericho Valley to keep his rendezvous with death.

Chapter Four

The sun was setting in scarlet and gold behind the gray wall of the Guadalupes when Walt Slade rode into Sotol. His face was lined and weary, but his eyes were bright, his carriage erect. Shadow's glossy coat was streaked with sweat and powdered with dust. However, he, too, showed no other signs of an exhaustive trek and a nerve shattering race with death.

In front of a weatherbeaten building, Slade pulled to a halt. Across the large window was legended, SHERIFF'S OFFICE — Clem Baxter, Sheriff.

As Slade looked at the building, which was unlighted and the door closed, a voice spoke pleasantly behind him, "Looking for somebody, cowboy?"

The sheriff's front window, with darkness behind it, provided a fair simulacrum of a mirror. In it Slade had watched the speaker approach, noting with interest that he wore a badge on his shirt front and that his holster was "tied down." He was a fairly tall man with a frank-looking face marked by keen eyes that were, like his hair, dark in contrast to his otherwise blond coloring.

Slade turned in his saddle and glanced down at the man as if seeing him for the first time. "Why, yes," he replied. "I was looking for the sheriff."

"He's not here," said the other. "Rode out of town a little while ago, over to one of the ranches west of here, I suppose. He didn't mention where he was going. Perhaps I'll do. I'm Clifton Yates, one of his deputies."

"Yes, I suppose you will," Slade conceded. "I just wanted to report that there are three dead men lying at the foot of the east wall of the big canyon about sixteen miles southeast of here on the Mojo Trail. And another one at the foot of the west wall right opposite."

The deputy's eyes widened. He recoiled a step and stared at Slade. "How's that again?" he asked, a bit dazedly it seemed to Slade. "Four dead men? How do you know they're dead?"

"Well, for one thing, if they aren't, they sure grew wings on the way down," Slade replied drily. "The wagon the three were riding is down there, too, smashed to flinders, and the horses to a pulp. They went over that five-hundred foot cliff."

"Good God!" gasped the deputy. "Horses ran away, I suppose."

"Yes, they ran away, all right," Slade conceded. "The horses were alive when they went over the cliff. The men were not."

Deputy Yates appeared utterly bewildered, which, Slade was forced to admit, was not unreasonable under the circumstances.

"Listen, cowboy, will you please explain what you're talking about?" he said.

Slade gave him the details of the tragedy on the Mojo. Yates listened with rigid attention. He licked his lips with a nervous tongue. "And you downed the one on top of the cliff?" he said. "Of course he was dead when you found him."

"I'd estimate it to be close to a thousand feet from that cliff top to the canyon floor," Slade replied obliquely.

Yates nodded. "And the wagon — did you notice what it was packing?"

"Flour and beans and grain scattered all over the canyon floor," Slade answered. "Appeared to be a provision wagon if one was to judge from the load."

"Uh-huh, but it might have been packing something else besides flour and beans," muttered the deputy. "That all you saw?"

"Yes, that's all, except a smashed rifle and an equally smashed sawed-off shotgun," Slade returned. "Do they guard flour and beans with scatterguns and Winchesters in this section?"

"No, they don't," grunted the deputy. "Uh-huh, you get the idea, all right. I'm willing to bet a hatful of pesos that somebody had gold in that wagon. Blast it! I wish the sheriff was here. He'd be pretty apt to know for sure, but he's close-mouthed and don't talk much to anybody. He sure didn't mention anything about a gold-packing wagon to me. Well, I suppose I'd better get a couple of the boys and ride down there. You coiling your twine here for a spell? 'Pears you're the only one who saw even part of what happened. We'll want you for the inquest." He hesitated, eyeing Slade speculatively.

Slade smiled down at him. "Remember, you don't know there are any bodies in that canyon," he said.

The deputy's eyes widened again. "What!" he exclaimed. "Why, you just told me there are!"

"Yes, but I could have been joking," Slade smiled. "You want to know before you think about locking me up."

The deputy flushed a little. "I didn't say

anything about locking you up," he growled.

"No, but that's what you were turning over in your mind," Slade stated.

Deputy Yates stared at him, then grinned, showing good teeth. "I told you I'm sort of new on this job," he said apologetically. "I don't know what to think. I'll look up Tom Horrel, he's been a deputy a long time, and see what he has to say."

Slade nodded. "A good notion," he answered. "Could you direct me to a livery stable and a place to sleep?"

"If you ride right around the next corner, just the other side of the Dun Cow saloon, you'll find a stable. Frank Nance, an old-timer, runs it and he's okay. Across from the stable is a rooming-house that I reckon is as good as any. Cowhands favor it. Nance runs it, too."

"Thanks," Slade said and gathered up his reins.

Again Yates seemed to hesitate. "By the way," he said, "did you happen to get a good look at those hellions down in the canyon? Think you'd know them if you saw them again?"

Slade shook his head. "At five-hundred feet, especially looking down into the shadows, faces are just a whitish blur," he explained. "Besides, I got just a glance at them before I had other things to think about, and when I next saw them they were riding up the canyon and several-hundred yards distant."

Yates nodded his understanding. "Be seeing you," he said and hurried away. Slade followed him with his gaze, his eyes fixed thoughtfully on the tied down holster.

Slade knew old-timers 'lowed that a man who wore the bottom of his holster strapped to his thigh never lived overly long after he began packing a gun. They insisted it was the trade mark of the professional gunfighter who sooner or later got his comeuppance, usually sooner.

Walt Slade, however, had his own theory. He had known peace officers who favored the arrangement. He held that the tie-down was a quick-draw man who was never quite sure of himself. A sure steady hand would pull a gun from its sheath without fear of dragging the sight against the leather, which was what the tie-down was supposed to guard against. The corollary, to Slade's way of thinking, was that the tie-down man still wasn't sure of himself after he cleared leather, which was the reason why he often fell victim to the man with greater confidence. Just a theory, he had to admit, but personal experience had proven him right on more than one occasion.

Slade located the livery stable without difficulty. Shadow was provided with comfortable quarters and all his wants cared for.

"Sure you can have a room," said the proprietor, who was a grizzled old-timer with a twinkle in his faded eyes. "Come on across and I'll fix you up."

Slade was satisfied with the plainly-furnished but clean room old Frank Nance showed him. He deposited his saddle pouches and rifle in a corner.

"Lock your door," Nance warned, handing him a key. "No, we ain't bothered with thievin'," he said with a chuckle at Slade's inquiring glance. "But if you don't, you liable to find some sociable gent in your bed when you aim to coil your twine for the night. The way they come, they just fall through the first unlocked door they find. Hey, who's down there?"

"How about a room for tonight, Pop?" replied a man in rangeland clothes and carrying a warbag, who had just entered the tiny office and was peering up the stairs.

"Yep, I got one left," said Nance. "Right next to this feller, only he shoots through the wall at gents that snores, just like John Wesley Hardin used to do," he added with a wink at Slade.

"Never heard myself snore," answered the new arrival, "so I reckon I can take a chance." He grinned, revealing crooked teeth badly tobacco-stained, and entered the room Nance pointed out, closing the door behind him.

"Sort of a mangy-lookin' critter, but you can't be too choosy in this business," Nance confided to Slade as they left the building. "Hope he doesn't snore."

"Chances are I wouldn't hear him, the way I sleep when I'm tired," Slade returned cheerfully. "Where's a good place to eat?"

"Good chuck at the Dun Cow," Nance replied. "You don't want to miss the Dun Cow. Fellers have been known to ride from clean down in the Davis Mountain country just to get a look at the Dun Cow. She's a lolapaloozer, all right. I've been as far west as California — spent quite a while there — and I ain't never seen anything to equal the Dun Cow, and hope I never will. Shows what kind of place a feller with delirium tremens can build."

As he turned the corner, Slade saw Deputy Clifton Yates and two other horsemen riding east in the fading light. Behind them rumbled a light wagon. Evidently they planned to bring the bodies back with them.

Slade agreed that the Dun Cow was all

his landlord claimed. Before leaving the roominghouse he had gotten a brief resume of the Dun Cow's history and he chuckled amusedly at old Sam Yelverton's conceit and his hankering for French windows.

Incidentally, the one old Ben Sutler rode his skewbald through had been replaced.

The French windows did not look so out of place in the new Sotol as they had before the metamorphosis took place. Nor did the big beamed room, nor the mirror blazing back bar crowded with bottles and the cedarwood front bar crowded with gentlemen interested in what the bottles contained.

Slade found a table and was soon eating an appetizing meal, but his eyes were as busy as his teeth. He had not failed to note the interest his entrance aroused in certain elements among the crowd at the bar and the gaming tables. Not an obvious interest — casual, a bit too casual — better described it. The kind of interest shown a stranger by men who were always thinking about what might happen if yesterday should catch up with today. Slade felt that there were quite a few of that sort in the Dun Cow. Yes, it was a salty pueblo, all right, and very likely the Dun Cow was the hub of the wheel.

He noticed that a counter had been rigged

up at the far end of the bar, upon which rested a set of delicately-balanced scales. Behind the scales presided a tall, sinewy man with a pleasant face and keen blue eyes. He was good looking, Slade thought, in a steely, polished way, with his alert eyes and think wavy hair of a pale ash color. He reminded Slade of somebody, but whom he could not at the moment recall.

From time to time a man in rough mining clothes would approach the counter and tender the tall man a plumped-out poke or two. The gold the pouches contained would be poured into the scale pan. The owner would be given a receipt which noted the weight of his nuggets and dust. Sometimes a sum in gold coins would also be handed him and the deduction noted on the receipt.

"Crane handles a good deal of the gold that comes out of Jericho Valley," said the waiter who had brought Slade his supper and noticed the direction of his glance remarked. "He ships it to Boraco, where the railroad takes it to the assay offices that buy it. Charges a mite more than the other shippers, but he uses more guards on his wagons and so far his shipments have always gotten through, which is more than can be said of some of the others."

"Crane?" Slade remarked interrogatively.

"Uh-huh, Crane Arnold. That's him behind the counter. He's the owner of this place. Bought it from old Sam Yelverton — that's Yelverton over at that poker game just this side of the faro bank, the old fat feller with the mustache and whiskers. He sold out to Crane because the place was making too darn much money and interfering with his poker and drinking. Some folks are sure hard to please!"

"Would seem that way," Slade smiled agreement and favored Yelverton with a keen glance. "Yelverton's an old-timer hereabouts, I presume?" he observed.

"Just about the oldest, except old Ben Butler, and nobody's seen Ben for quite a spell now, and I reckon that makes Yelverton the oldest," the waiter explained. "It was Ben who first discovered the gold in Jericho Valley. Him and Sam were pretty good friends. Sam likes to talk about him when he's feeling his likker. Reckon he'll be feeling it before long, now, the way he's downing it this evening. He's winning at poker and feeling good. Sociable gent, old Sam."

CHAPTER FIVE

Slade finished his meal and rolled a cigarette. There was a vacant spot at the end of the bar next to the gold-weighing counter. Lighting his cigarette, he strolled over and occupied it.

The bartender who served him was a sociable sort, one of Sam Yelverton's old-timers. He welcomed Slade and indulged in conversation as he poured a drink.

"Stranger hereabouts, ain't you, son?" he asked.

" 'Pears everybody hits this section sooner or later," he replied to Slade's affirmative nod. "This is, since Ben Sutler found gold in Jericho Valley. You figuring on hitting the diggings? Not much that hasn't already been staked out, that is all that looks good, but you never can tell about such things. Might be some mighty good ground left that don't show much on the surface."

"Might take a whirl at it, can't say for

sure," Slade equivocated. "I'm more of a cowhand that a miner, though."

"Take my advice and stick to riding," offered the barkeep. "Me, I wouldn't prowl into that snake hole up there for all the gold in it."

"Bad section?"

"Bad ain't no name for it. Those cliffs that wall the valley are all busted and shattered. Water gets in back of the rocks every time it rains and big hunks of 'em come tumbling down when you're least expecting it. In winter they just aren't safe a minute. A loud word will bring them down and whole rafts of snow that clings to the cliffs let go. There won't be any mining much up there come cold weather. It's one goshawful place. If you sit down, a rattler bites you. If you take a drink from a spring, like as not it's arsenic water and you cash in with pains like a hydrophobia skunk gnawing his way through your belly. But the boys keep bringing in nuggets and dust, and so long as that's so I reckon the darn fools will keep on risking the snakes and the poison water and the falling rocks."

Slade sipped his drink, meanwhile surveying the activities of the big room in the back-bar mirrors. Those mirrors were set at all angles, so that a man standing at the bar could see all parts of the room without turning his head. After a while he left the bar and strolled over to where Sam Yelverton and his cronies, several elderly, keen-eyed cattlemen, were wrangling over their cards.

For some minutes Slade stood watching the game. Old Sam glanced up, caught his eye and waved a hospitable hand.

"Set in, cowboy, if you're so minded," he invited, nodding to a vacant chair. The other players glanced at Slade, then nodded agreement.

The stakes were not large, but the players showed a real zest for the game. Slade, who liked poker, was thoroughly enjoying himself. He held his own, even won a little, playing his cards with a shrewdness that gained him approving nods from his elderly opponents.

"I like this young feller," old Sam declared with emphasis. "Hope you'll stick around, son, and if you're looking for work you won't have any trouble finding it, eh, Wes?"

The cowman addressed nodded. "Roundup time is just around the corner and the spreads have been losing quite a few hands of late," he said. "The boys have been getting the gold fever since the strike up in Jericho Valley."

"Dadblast that infernal gold strike!"

growled old Sam. "It's cost the lives of too many good men, including poor old Ben Sutler. Don't you go falling for it, son. That kind of money doesn't ever do a feller any good. Look at those loco jugheads at the bar — throwing away in one night what it's took them a week of risking their lives to get."

Prompted by an adroit question or two from Slade, Yelverton began talking. Soon the cards lay neglected, the subject being of interest to all present, and before long Slade got the whole of the story of Ben Sutler and his strike.

"And you figure Sutler is dead?" he asked old Sam.

Yelverton hesitated and before he made up his mind how to answer, the cattleman Wes Hargrove put in a few words.

"I can't figure anything else but a harp or a coal shovel would keep Ben Sutler away from the Dun Cow and poker and whiskey," he said. "Yes, that blasted snake hole must have gotten poor Ben. But what became of his body is past me. We hunted and hunted but weren't able to find hide or hair of him."

"One of those rock slides would bury a feller so you'd never find him," another cattleman observed.

"Doesn't look like it would bury his horse,

too," objected Hargrove. "That darn skewbald vanished from sight, too, and it would never have left Ben, even if he was dead."

"Some mighty big slides and rock falls happen up there," persisted the other cattleman.

"Guess maybe you're right," Hargrove admitted.

Sam Yelverton finally spoke up. "Gents, I know it sounds crazy, but I've said it before and I'm saying it again, I don't believe Ben Sutler is dead. I just feel he ain't."

"But where the devil is he if he isn't dead?" demanded Hargrove.

"I don't know, but just the same I got a feeling he ain't dead," Yelverton said.

And for no reason he could put his finger on, Walt Slade experienced a feeling of agreement with old Sam. And an equally nonsensical feeling that in some way the mystery of Ben Sutler's disappearance was tied up with the mystery he, Slade, had been sent into the section to solve — the mystery of who was responsible for the depredations that had been plaguing Sotol and the surrounding country.

"Oh, heck! Let's have a drink and forget it," said Yelverton. "I'm finished with cards for tonight."

The others agreed and after the drink they

trooped off to bed. Slade returned to the bar, finding a place not far from the weighing counter. Crane Arnold caught his eye and nodded pleasantly, smiling in a friendly fashion. Arnold was undoubtedly a good host.

The hour was late, well past midnight, but business was still booming. It was evident that a goodly portion of the gold of Jericho Valley found its way into the tills of the Dun Cow.

Suddenly the babble of conversation at the bar died down somewhat; men glanced over their shoulders. Slade, who stood hal facing the swinging doors, his gaze fixed on the back-bar mirror, saw a remarkable-looking individual making his way from the entrance to the bar.

The newcomer was a huge man with slightly bowed shoulders, long, dangling arms and blunt-fingered hairy hands. He had a tight slit of a mouth, a big chin and sultry eyes. He paused for a moment to greet an acquaintance in a harsh, rumbling voice.

"That's Russ Berry who owns the Root Hog, best paying claim in Jericho Valley," the bartender who served him whispered to Slade. "A salty hombre and something of a troublemaker. Had a row with three fellers in here one night not long ago. Whupped 'em all three before you could say 'scat'! One of the fellers went for his gun, but Russ blowed a hole through his arm before he could clear leather. Tarnation fast for a big man, though you wouldn't figure it to look at him."

After a few words with his acquaintance Russ Berry made his way to the gold-weighing counter. Crane Arnold nodded shortly in reply to his greeting. Berry drew three plump pokes from his capacious pockets and Arnold began adjusting his scales. The gold was dumped into the pan, filling it several times. Berry meanwhile talked to Arnold in low tones Slade could not catch. The saloonkeeper's eyes narrowed a trifle and an irritated look passed across his face. He replied apparently in monosyllables.

"Crane ain't got much use for Berry," the bartender remarked. "Berry's a good spender and Crane handles his shipments, so he sort of tolerates him, but I've a notion he'd be just as pleased if Berry stayed away. After Berry had the rukus in here, Crane told him that if he got into any more trouble he'd be barred from the Dun Cow. Berry grumbled, but he didn't talk back to Crane. Arnold's quiet and talks soft and is easy to get along with, but I figure he could be plenty salty himself if necessary. He was head dealer here before he bought the place and I reckon he was a dealer most of his life, and those card dealers ain't exactly easy to push around."

"Looks efficient, all right," Slade agreed.

"He's that," replied the bartender. "Nice feller to work for — I never worked for a nicer. Give him what's coming to him and he'll back you till the last brand's run. Russ Berry is about the only jigger I ever saw him get rough with."

The weighing finished, Berry got his receipt and slouched to a table, sat down and ordered a drink which he downed in a gulp and demanded another.

It seemed to Slade that something was bothering the big fellow, for his brow knotted querulously, his lips moved as if he were muttering to himself and from time to time he shot a glowering look toward the end of the bar where Crane Arnold stood. Slade reasoned that he might be irritated at something Arnold had said to him.

However, his irritation did not express itself beyond scowls and inaudible mutters. A few minutes later a man detached himself from the crowd at the bar and sauntered over to Berry's table. Slade had no trouble following the conversation that followed.

"Must have had a good week, Russ," the other remarked.

"Plumb good," Berry rumbled harshly. "The farther back we get the richer the dirt gets. If we can just keep the blasted cliff from tumbling down on top of us we should do fine. Looks mighty bad of late, though, mighty bad. I heard a slide let loose to the north of my claim just before I saddled up for town. Sounded like a big one. If it hadn't been so dark I'd have ridden up to see what happened. Might have caught somebody, but I didn't hear any yelling."

"Not liable to, if it did catch somebody," the other man observed grimly. "Those slides don't leave a jigger much to yell with when they catch him."

Berry nodded and gulped his drink. "Be seeing you, Bob," he said and clumped out, his muddy boots pounding the floor purposefully. Slade followed his broad back with his eyes. Berry looked to be a hard character, all right, but Slade thought that he also looked rather stupid.

A little later Slade also left the saloon and headed for the little roominghouse on the side street. Aside from a light burning in the tiny office and another in the hall above, the building was in darkness. Slade chuckled as he opened the front door. Looked like he was the only occupant with going-to-bed notions. Apparently everybody else in Sotol resolved to see the sun up, if by then they'd be in a condition to see anything.

A light also burned in the stable across the street. Doubtless the old proprietor, Frank Nance, was busy with some late chores.

With a quick, lithe step, Slade mounted the stairs and walked down the dimly lighted hall. He fumbled the old-fashioned key from his pocket and thrust it into the keyhole, reflecting the while that most any door key would very likely fit the clumsy lock. He turned the key, reached for the doorknob and abruptly jerked his hand back as if the thing were redhot.

They key had turned easily — too easily; there was no pressure against it, and there was no tiny grating of the moving bolt. Still holding the key, Slade stared at the closed door. The answer to the unusual behavior of the key was that the door wasn't locked, and he knew very well he had locked it upon leaving the room a few hours before.

And what was the answer to that? Perhaps Nance had come back to the room for some reason and on leaving had forgotten to shoot the bolt. That, however, seemed unlikely, seeing as he had cautioned his guest to be sure and lock the door after going out. But somebody had unlocked it, ostensibly to enter the room. The third and most important question, to which Slade didn't have the answer, was whether somebody was in the room right now? And if so, why? His life might depend on that answer. People didn't unlock doors and enter another's room with good intentions in mind, at least very rarely.

Slade stood perfectly still, listening. If somebody was in the room he had assuredly heard him approach the door and thrust the key into the keyhole. And if he was waiting for El Halcon to enter, he would naturally try not to make a sound. But also he would be under a certain amount of nervous strain and it is hard for a nervous person to keep from moving, no matter how little, and Slade's keen ears would catch the sound of that movement, slight though it might be.

Slowly the minutes passed, and nothing happened. If the possible intruder was also playing a waiting game, he was playing it well. Something had to be done. Slade reached out, grasped the doorknob and, standing well to one side, turned it by infinitesimal degrees. Finally the turning knob halted; the catch was shot. With a quick jerk Slade swung the door wide open, ducking back as he did so.

There was a blinding flash and a crashing roar. Buckshot screeched through the opening and slammed against the wall. Slade jumped farther back, a gun in each hand, and stood motionless.

When his ears stopped ringing he could still hear no sound inside the room. It was silent as a tomb. Across the street the stable door banged open. Evidently old Frank had heard the shooting and placed it. Slade heard the pad of his feet crossing the street. He slipped his hat from his head, balanced it on the end of his gun barrel and thrust it forward to simulate somebody peering quickly around the door jamb. And still nothing happened. Nance's voice came from the office.

"What the devil's going on up there," he called.

"Bring a lamp and come up," Slade called back, his eyes never leaving the dark opening.

Nance's boots sounded on the stairs. From the corner of his eye Slade saw him hurrying down the corridor, a cocked gun in one hand, a lamp in the other.

"Careful," Slade warned. "Stay out of line

with that door."

Nance halted as if he had been shot. By the bar of light streaming down the hall, Slade saw what he had missed in the semi-gloom. From the inner doorknob dangled a length of stout string. He began to understand. "Easy," he cautioned Nance. "Hand me the lamp."

Holding the lamp well to the front, he took a chance and peered into the room. As he expected, it was without occupancy. His eyes fixed on the devilish contraption that had been rigged up to kill him when he opened the door.

Lashed to the bedpost was a sawed-off shotgun. A length of string similar to that fastened to the doorknob hung down around the stock. One end had been tightly tied to the triggers of the shotgun.

"See how it works?" he remarked to the astounded proprietor. "String tied to the triggers passed around the stock and across the room to the doorknob. With the door opening outward, the tightening of the string pulled the triggers and whoever was coming in would have gotten a double charge of blue whistlers dead center. Look what they did to your wall!"

Old Frank gulped and goggled. "How'd they miss you?" he asked.

"When I found the door unlocked, I thought it a bit funny, seeing that I was sure I locked it going out," Slade explained. "So when I opened it I was careful to stand out of line."

"But why should anybody do such a thing —" Nance began. He broke off, regarded Slade a bit strangely. "What you been mixed up in, son?" he asked.

Slade reflected a moment, then gave him a brief account of what happened on the Mojo Trail.

"That's it," Nance immediately decided. "They got a look at you, spotted you when you rode into town and were out to even up the score, the snake-blooded hellions! Some bad characters in this section."

"So it would appear," Slade agreed.

"But how did they work it — how'd they get in?" Nance wondered.

"Suppose we take a look in the next room," Slade suggested.

Nance opened the door, which was not locked. The room was empty, the bed had not been slept in and there were a couple of cigarette butts on the floor. Nance glared about suspiciously.

"You figure that ratty-looking hellion who rented this one did it?"

"I don't know," Slade admitted, adding

dryly, "but I'm ready to bet a flock of pesos that you don't see him again. I suppose you gave him a key, too?" Nance nodded. "And most any key with a little manipulating would very likely unlock any room in the place. He waited till you went back to the stable, slipped into my room, rigged up his contraption and slid out and away, or at least that's the way I figure it. He made one little slip, as the owlhoot brand usually does — he forgot to lock the door before he high-tailed, and that saved me. Lucky you didn't take a notion to come back up for something."

Nance shivered. "And I've often done just that," he said. "To put in another blanket if it seemed to be getting cool, or to make sure a jigger didn't leave a butt burning on the floor."

"Well, it worked out okay and that's all that counts," Slade said as they returned to his room. He cut the shotgun loose from the bedpost and handed it to Nance.

"Souvenir for you," he said. "Tomorrow you can spend the day picking buckshot out of the wall. I'm going to bed."

"You going to sleep?" snorted Nance. "Me, I'd be settin' up all night with a gun in each fist and a knife between my teeth."

"Guess nothing more will happen tonight," Slade laughed. "I don't think the gent will come back to see if his scatter-gun was aimed straight."

"I wish he would and give me a chance to line sights with him, the lowdown, mangy son of a hydrophobia skunk! Well, good night. See you in the morning, I hope."

Slade locked the door, leaving the key in the lock. He knew nobody could jiggle that key out without awakening him. Then he went to bed in no very good temper.

His anger was directed chiefly at himself and his own stupidity. A clumsy trap had been laid for him in a time-worn and clumsy manner, and he had escaped walking into it through sheer luck. Looking back, he could see that, circumstances and conditions being what they were, he should have been suspicious of the unsavory character who had practically followed him into the roominghouse, of course with spotting the room he would occupy in mind. But he didn't give the fellow a thought, noting him so casually that he doubted if he'd recognize him if he met him in the street. Well, he had come close to paying dearly for his carelessness.

"Seems getting into a blasted town addles my think tank," he grumbled to the lamp as he extinguished it. "Out in the open I'd have noticed how many hairs that hellion had in his left eyebrow!"

Several times during the night Slade heard some fatigued roisterer stumbling down the hall to bed, but nobody approached his door and it was the sun shining brightly through the window that finally awakened him. Feeling much refreshed he dressed and crossed to the stable to make sure Shadow was okay.

"Nothing else happened, eh?" remarked old Frank Nance who was pottering about and cleaning the stalls. "Trough in the back if you'd like a dip, and there's a razor and soap on the shelf under the looking glass. Help yourself."

Slade enjoyed a shave and a sluice in the cold water, after which he repaired to the Dun Cow for a late breakfast. He was eating with appetite when Deputy Clifton Yates, old Sam Yelverton and the cattleman Wes Hargrove entered. They spotted Slade and approached his table. Yelverton and the cowman regarded him with quickened interest.

"Just as I figured," Yates announced. "That infernal wagon was packing a gold shipment sent out by Jasper Gould." He eyed Slade a moment. "And you're sure you didn't get a look at those hellions, and they were all gone when you got down to the canyon floor?" he asked.

"That's what I told you yesterday, I believe," Slade replied. Yates hesitated again and was about to ask another question when Sam Yelverton interrupted him.

"Tighten your cinches, Cliff," he said. "You ain't got no call to be insinuating this feller might have had something to do with what happened. If he had, why the devil would he have ridden into town and told you all about it first off, and you the Law? Does that make sense?"

Yates flushed and he hastened to disavow the charge, "I ain't insinuating anything about anybody," he declared. "I just know that somebody got away with twenty-thousand dollars in dust and nuggets and Jasper Gould gave me Old Harry. Seemed to feel I was to blame for the whole thing. I'm sorry, Slade, and I didn't mean it the way it sounded. And take my advice and don't never get mixed up with peace officerin' if you don't want to end up plumb loco. Where the devil did the sheriff get to? I figured he'd be back long before now. We'll hold an inquest in about an hour, Slade, and I reckon you should be present."

"I'll be there," Slade promised. The last thing he heard as Yates and his companions departed was the deputy's resumed plaint over Sheriff Baxter's unexplained absence.

Chapter Six

The sun was behind the Guadalupes when Sheriff Clem Baxter rode into Jericho Valley the evening before, and the great gorge was already brimful of shadows.

Jericho Valley was really nothing but a wide, very long and winding canyon walled by shattered cliffs and almost perpendicular shale slopes. Old Testament Tillotson, a wandering evangelist, had named Jericho Canyon. Old Testament, who combined religion with prospecting, wandered into the canyon in company of another prospector of misty antecedents. It was autumn and before they were up the gorge a mile a rock fall came within a frog's hair of wiping them out. Loosened by the vibrations set up by the first, a second slide roared down two hundred yards farther up canyon. Old Testament stared at the rolling boulders and sliding shale and wagged his white beard.

"Just like the walls of Jericho when Joshua

blowed his trumpet," Old Testament 'lowed. " 'And the walls came tumblin' down!' Uh-huh, just like Jericho. Samp, we'll just name her Jericho Valley."

The other prospector was not inclined to argue the point, and after just missing drinking from an arsenic spring, and escaping snakebite only because the rattler in question was torpid with cold, Old Testament and Samp decided to get away from there. Otherwise they might have discovered the gold Ben Sutler stumbled onto forty years later. From that time on, until Sutler's time, Jericho Valley was pretty much left alone.

A beaten track paralleled the east wall of the canyon, but Sheriff Baxter did not follow it.

Instead, he threaded his way through the brush and rock a half mile or more west of the route taken by the miners in their trips to and from town. He could see, through the tangle of growth, the occasional lights of cabins or leantos that provided some shelter for the claim workers and he knew each light marked the site of a nearby tunnel boring into the uncertain shale banks below the cliffs. He was several miles up the canyon before he pulled up in a thicket that flanked a trickle of water. Here he hobbled his horse where the cayuse could find plenty to eat and drink. Then, loosening his old Smith-Wesson in its sheath, he stole across the canyon toward a yellow rectangle of light that marked a cabin somewhat larger and more commodious than any he had yet passed.

Sheriff Baxter did not approach the cabin. He carefully skirted it, pausing to listen from time to time. Apparently satisfied with what he did not see or hear, he crept on toward the swell of a huge shale bank that stretched its steeply sloping extent to the rim of the canyon. With many a pause to peer and listen, he slowly made his way toward a darker shadow discovering itself in the gloom. A few more steps and the shadow resolved into a black opening in the bank. It was the mouth of a mine tunnel.

With infinite caution, his right hand hovering over the butt of his gun, the old peace officer approached the opening. On the threshold he paused again, peering, listening. He cast a glance back toward the lighted cabin, hesitated an instant longer, then stepped boldly into the tunnel mouth. Another pace or two and suddenly he floundered, tripped and fell. As he strove to rise, a grinding roar sounded over his head. With a rending crash a huge section of broken rock crashed down. There was a thin, horrible sound for an instant, like the anguished squeal of a rat squashed under the bar of a weighted trap, then silence. Without sound or motion Sheriff Baxter lay with his head and the upper portion of his body buried beneath a mass of earth and broken stone.

The crash of the falling rocks shattered the silence of the valley like a thunderclap. Scarcely had the echoes died away when sound arose from the nearby lighted cabin. There was the scrape of pushed back chairs, the clump of booted feet hitting the floor. A moment later a door creaked on its hinges. The light in the cabin went out.

Another short space of silence, then there sounded the stealthy scuff of boots on the flinty soil. Shadows stole from the darkness, approached the tunnel mouth. The shadows resolved into the figures of three men.

The foremost, who strode forward, gun in hand, was a huge man with slightly-bowed shoulders and long, gorilla-like arms. He paused to listen, then gestured to his companions and glided forward again, amazingly light on his feet for so large a man. Just outside the tunnel mouth he halted, his head trust forward on his neck.

"Got him — a blasted prowler!" he exclaimed in a harsh, rumbling voice.

"Who the devil is it, Russ?" asked one of the two men crowding behind him.

"How the devil do I know — do you think I can see in the dark?" the giant growled. "Strike a light. You brought the lantern, didn't you?"

There was a scraping sound, a match flared. A steady glow lighted the scene as the flame was touched to the lantern wick.

"Haul him out," ordered the big man, gesturing toward the legs of the prostrate figure under the fallen stone.

Grunting and puffing, his two companions began to move chunks of rock. One labored clumsily with only his left hand. His right was thrust into the front of his shirt and he tenderly cherished his right arm. With an impatient oath the big man shoved him aside. Under his great hands ponderous lumps of stone flew aside as if they were pebbles.

"The hellion got just the outside of the fall," rumbled the big man. "Most of the stuff fell inside the tunnel, but he got enough, I reckon."

Another moment and the limp, broken form was hauled free. The lantern was held to the battered face.

"Good God!" gasped one of the men. "It's

the sheriff!"

A moment of stunned silence followed. Then the second man, who had as yet not spoken, exclaimed in a shaking, querulous voice, "Now ain't this the end! Cashed in the sheriff! You and your smart notion of setting up a deadfall to catch a prowler, Russ Berry! Now we are in one devil of a mess. Killing sheriffs is mighty bad business in this country."

Russ Berry had for the moment been as appalled by the discovery as were his companions, but he quickly recovered his aplomb and turned fiercely on the speaker. "You blasted loco wind spider!" he rasped. "What if it is the sheriff? Can't you see what it means? Baxter caught onto something, how, the devil only knows, but he must have. If he didn't, why would he come sneaking into our tunnel in the dark? Answer me that, will you? And if he did catch onto something, where would we stand? This is the very best thing that could have happened. Clem Baxter was almighty good at keeping his trap shut. I'll bet money he didn't tell anybody else what he found out, not yet. Now he's done for and we're safe."

"But when they find him dead in our tunnel, then what?" the other quavered.

Russ Berry swore with bitter scorn. "Do I

have to think of eveything for both of you?" he demanded exasperatedly. "Who's going to find him here? Nobody. Who's going to know he was killed here? Nobody!"

"How you going to work it, Russ?" the first speaker asked eagerly.

"Pack him up the canyon and drop him at the foot of that big slope a quarter of a mile to the north," explained Berry. "Some of the miners up there will find him tomorrow, and it'll look like he was fooling around up top the canyon rim and fell over. That's happened to folks before now. The slope's almost straight up-and-down and a feller would be sure to bust his neck if he rolled down there. Me and Courtney will pack him up there. Bayles, you scout around till you find his horse. He'd have been most liable to leave the critter over by the crik bank and not far off. Slide into the thickets over there and you'll find it. Take it up top the cliffs — you know how to get up — and turn it loose there close to the big slope. You can do that much even if you have got a hole in your blasted arm. They'll find the horse when they come looking tomorrow. He won't stray far and it'll make the thing look plumb authentic. Get a move on. Take the lantern with you but douse it till you get behind the thickets. Somebody might come riding this way from one of the claims up the canyon and you don't want anybody clapping an eye on you. All right, get going. Come on, Courtney, you'll make out so long as you don't have to sit down. What I can't understand is why that slug didn't blow your blasted brains out."

"Hit a mite low for that," Courtney replied, tenderly caressing the region of his hip pocket.

"Not for my money it didn't," grunted Berry. "Let's go!"

Together, Berry and Courtney carried the body up the canyon, their way lighted by the faint gleam of the stars. At the foot of a steep and towering slope of cracked rock, they laid it down amid a welter of boulders and broken stone.

"Nobody would figure anything but that he went over the lip up there," Russ Berry declared with satisfaction. "Come on, let's get back to the shack. I'm riding to town right away with our cleanup. I think it's a good idea to let folks in town see me tonight."

"But what about our tunnel mouth — all caved in?" asked Courtney. "I've a notion from the looks of it that a sight more of the roof came down than what you had balanced up there to fall if somebody walked into that rope stretched across the tunnel."

"We'll take care of it tomorrow," said Berry. "Wouldn't look good if somebody happened along and saw us working on it tonight. Tomorrow it'll be different. Rock falls are too common in this section for anybody to think anything of them. Yes, I figure everything will be okay, Baxter being out of the way won't do us no harm."

Chapter Seven

The news of the gold-wagon robbery spread swiftly, and before Slade finished his breakfast, groups of men were crowding into the saloon, animatedly discussing the outrage. Curious glances were cast at Walt Slade but nobody approached him.

Slade smoked a leisurely cigarette, glanced at the clock and decided he might as well repair to the sheriff's office, where preparations for the inquest would be getting underway.

When he reached the office, he found it already pretty well filled. Doc Beard, the coroner, was making ready to select a jury. Slade joined Sam Yelverton and Wes Hargrove. With them was a keen-eyed little man who was introduced as Tom Horrel, one of Sheriff Baxter's deputies.

The jury was impanelled and the inquest was about to start when a most unexpected diversion occurred. Down the street from the direction of Jericho Valley a wild-eyed rider spurred a foaming horse. He jerked his mount to a sliding halt in front of the office and let out a yell.

"The sheriff!" he bawled. "Sheriff Baxter's dead! He's laying up in the valley 'neath a slope, all busted to hell, his neck broke and everything!"

There was a moment of paralyzed inaction, then the crowd boiled out of the office shouting oaths and questions. Old Wes Hargrove, who was a county commissioner, took charge of the situation.

"Get your horse, Yates," he directed. "We'll ride up there. Come along, Sam, and you, too, Slade. Horrel, you bring a lead horse to pack the body back."

From Sotol to Jericho Valley was about two hours' fair riding, but the posse made it in considerably less time. Miners of the claims inside the valley paused from work to stare at them as they rode past.

Walt Slade swept the wide canyon with an interested gaze. And before long he arrived at a conclusion which it appeared neither the miners nor the Sotol business men who talked of and planned for the future realized.

Before joining the Texas Rangers, Walt Slade had graduated from a well-known college of engineering. He had planned to take a post-graduate course to round out his education before settling down to the profession for which he had been trained. But the loss of his father's ranch, due to droughts, blizzards and widelooping activities, and the subsequent untimely death of the elder Slade had made that impossible at the time. So when Captain Jim McNelty, with whom Slade had worked some during summer vacations, suggested that he sign up with the Rangers for a while and pursue his studies in his spare time, Slade had acceded. Long ago he had gotten more from private study than he could have hoped to glean from the postgrad course, but Ranger work had gotten a strong hold on him and he was reluctant to sever relations with the famous corps of law enforcement officers. He was young and there was plenty of time. He'd eventually become an engineer but for the present he'd stick with the Rangers.

As a result of his knowledge of such matters, Walt Slade now viewed Jericho Valley with the eye of a geologist and knew there would be no future of wealth and continued prosperity for Sotol. Here was no inexhaustible store of riches. The Ashes Mountains, of which Jericho Valley was an integral part, were the result of a volcanic upheaval. The cliffs were basaltic and therefore plutonic. In truth, nothing but cooled and weathered lava that had poured forth from earth heart in the dim past. Here were no ledges of gold bearing quartz, no fabulous Mother Lode extending indefinitely into the hills. Jericho Valley had once been, untold ages ago, the bed of a river. The gold of Jericho Valley was an alluvial deposit brought from perhaps hundreds of miles distant by the rushing waters of the stream whose course had been changed by the terrestrial convulsion that formed the Ashes Mountains, and the deposits were strictly limited. Only along the lower gravel basing the shale banks, which had once been under water would gold be found. The upper slopes were barren of metal. In fact, Slade shrewdly suspected that the treasure of the valley was already very nearly exhausted. Soon the claims would be worthless.

He wondered if there were not some experienced placer and pocket miners present who would have read the signs aright. Very likely there were not, he reflected. The Jericho Valley strike had been a purely local affair and all the productive ground had quickly been staked. The miners were former cowhands, teamsters, town folks from Sotol and adjacent communities.

The strike had not been extensive enough to attract prospectors from afar. In Texas, in contrast to California and Nevada, for example, placer and pocket mining were rare. Here was one of the few exceptions.

Yes, mining in Jericho Valley would soon come to an end. Which result would seriously affect his plans. He had been sent into the section as a Texas Ranger to run down certain malefactors and bring them to justice. As long as gold was mined in Jericho Valley and prosperity remained at a high level they would very likely continue their unsavory operations; but when the claims petered out they would drift away to inflict their unwelcome presence on some other community. Time was running out.

A short distance above, a larger than average cabin set close to the trail and the creek that ran beyond it, the posse paused for a moment opposite a tunnel mouth where Russ Berry and two more men were busy clearing away a rock fall that choked the tunnel mouth.

Russ Berry desisted from his labors and walked over to speak with the posse. He directed his words at Chief Deputy Yates.

"He's layin' right at the foot of that big sag just north of here," Berry said. "Smashed up something awful. The only way I can figure it is he lost his way up top the slope and unforked to hunt for a trail. Must have gotten too close to the edge in the dark and it caved in with him. Some of the boys found his horse a little while ago. Was grazing up there, reins broke and trailing. I was busy with that blasted fall that blocked our tunnel last night but when a feller brought the word of what happened, I hustled up the canyon for a look and saw what was left of him. I told the boys not to touch him, that the coroner would like as not want to see him right the way he was found. Howdy, Doc, see you came along. I did right, didn't I?"

"Guess you did," admitted the coroner. "All right, boys, let's go."

They found what was left of Sheriff Baxter lying amid a scattering of rocks and boulders at the foot of the towering slope. The back of his head had been completely bashed in, his neck broken, his shirt ripped to shreds and his back and shoulders smashed to pulp.

"Poor old Clem," muttered Sam Yelverton, "he's a mess. I wonder what in tarnation he was doing up top that darn sag?"

"Must have come down end over end," grunted Doc Beard, the coroner, peering with near-sighted eyes at the corpse. "Gosh!

he's busted up awful."

Walt Slade was gazing at the sheriff's boots. They were good boots and almost brand-new, even the soles were hardly scuffed. He shifted his glance to the long slope studded with boulders and fragments of loose stone, dropped it to the ground where the body lay.

There were plenty of boulders and loose stones scattered about. Slade carelessly shoved one aside with his toe. The underside revealed insect life scurrying for cover. He moved a second one, and a third, with like results. He sauntered around to the other side of the body, over which his companions were still exclaiming, their attention centered on the grisly remains. Two more stones displayed moist under-surfaces and agitated bugs. Slade again studied the sheriff's boots, and again raised his glance to the slope. He turned and gazed down the sinister valley, his eyes cold and subtly changed in color.

"Well, guess we'd better load him on the spare horse and take him back to town," Deputy Yates remarked sadly. "Looks like you'll hold a double-barreled inquest tomorrow, Doc."

The other posse members discussed the sheriff's death and his past life at length as they rode back to Sotol, but Walt Slade was singularly silent, gazing straight ahead of him for the most part, the concentration furrow deep between his black brows. Only once did he really turn his head for any length of time. It was when they passed the blocked tunnel mouth where Russ Berry and his helpers had resumed work. For a long moment he regarded the mass of broken stone and the busy toilers.

Slade was, in fact, too busy with his own thoughts to do any talking. For the second time that day he had noted what apparently everybody else missed. And what he had seen convinced him that Sheriff Baxter had not fallen from the canyon rimrock. Indeed, Slade doubted if he had ever been up there at all.

Sheriff Baxter had been killed by a rock fall, all right. The condition of his body was ample proof of that, but not by rocks pounding him as he rolled down the steep slope. Of that Slade was convinced, with plenty of obvious evidence to bolster up his conviction.

In the first place, there was not a sign of scratching or scuffing on the new boots the sheriff wore. The leather was smooth and glossy, which it could not have possibly remained after a roll down the rock-studded surface of the long slope. Additionally, his riding britches showed no tears or smudges. Secondly, where the sheriff lay there were no recently fallen stones. Boulders and fragments of rock would have inevitably been dislodged by his progress down the slope. All the stones around the body had been there long enough to provide sanctuary for insect life.

The answer? Sheriff Baxter had been killed elsewhere and his body moved to the spot where it was found!

But why and by whom was not so easy to explain. There had been a rock fall in the mouth of Russ Berry's mine tunnel. But what business could the sheriff have had in that tunnel, and why would Berry drop rocks on his head and kill him? Two more questions to which there were no obvious answers. Of course there was nothing resembling evidence that the sheriff was killed in Berry's tunnel. The fact that there had been a rock fall in the tunnel the night before meant little. Rock falls in Jericho Valley, in the mine tunnels and elsewhere, were of common occurrence. Doubtless just a not at all remarkable coincidence that one had occurred in Berry's tunnel the same night the sheriff was killed by one. But the peace officer had been killed, and somebody had transported his body from where he was killed to the bottom of the slope. And Slade had a feeling, based on little more than intuition and experience with dubious characters, that there might be something off-color about Russ Berry. At least he was something to concentrate on till something more promising showed up.

Slade was still pondering the problem when they reached Sotol. He stabled his horse and repaired to the Dun Cow for something to eat.

The robbery of the gold-bearing wagon and the death of Sheriff Baxter gave the town plenty to talk about that night. The air was filled with wild conjectures and wilder rumors. Everybody appeared to have an opinion to express and expressed it long and loud. Slade finally grew weary of the continuous uproar and went to bed. He reached his room without incident and slept soundly.

The double inquest was to be held the following afternoon and it was a foregone conclusion that the jury's verdict would be that Sheriff Baxter's death was due to a deplorable accident. Nobody, least of all Walt Slade, suspected the astounding denouement that would dramatize what promised to be a hundrum affair.

The inquest got underway on schedule.

The murdered driver and guards of the gold wagon were disposed of first. The verdict read that they had met their deaths at the hands of parties unknown and a "rider" advised the deputies to get off the seat of their pants and bring the sidewinders in for a hanging. Which rider occasioned muttered profanity from said deputies. Next came the man Slade shot off the cliff top, an unencouraging spectacle with his face smashed out of all semblance to a human countenance, which Slade regretted. Otherwise somebody might have recognized him and remembered with whom he associated. Slade was quickly absolved of blame in the killing and the hope expressed that he might get a chance to line sights with some more of the varmints.

Finally the death of Sheriff Baxter was considered, a mere formality, for it was already conceded by all that his death had been accidental. The verdict was being worded when the proceedings were interrupted by a clatter of hoofs outside. Glancing through the window, Slade saw Russ Berry and his two partners, Bayles and Courtney, pulling their horses to a halt in front of the building. Bayles and Courtney remained in their saddles, their faces wearing an apprehensive expression, but Berry slowly dismounted. For a moment he seemed to hesitate, then he squared his shoulders and marched into the office. He removed his hat and fumbled it in his big hands. He took a deep breath.

"Gents," he said, "I've got something I'd like to say. Is it all right?"

"Why, sure, Russ, what's on your mind?" Doc Cooper replied wonderingly.

Berry took another deep breath, fumbled his hat. "Gents, I've got a confession to make," he burst out. "I killed the sheriff!"

Chapter Eight

There followed a silence of utter astonishment. Men stared at Berry as if convinced he had suddenly gone insane.

"Yes, I killed him," Berry repeated heavily, "but I didn't mean to, God knows I didn't. It happened this way. As all of you know, us fellers up in the valley have had a lot of trouble with ore thieves. A couple of hellions can sneak into a tunnel at night and dig out a lot of metal, especially if they happen to hit a rich pocket. It's happened to several of the boys and it happened to me once. You can't work a claim all day and sit up and guard it all night. So I got what I figured was a bright notion. I rigged up a deadfall in the mouth of my tunnel, with some big rocks balanced so they'd come tumbling down on any varmint who butted into a rope stretched across the bore to trip the trap. Well, that's what happened to the sheriff. He must have butted into the rope and the rocks came down, and brought a whole section of the roof with them. Reckon he never knew what hit him."

Again there was a stunned silence, then a rising babble of exclamations and questions. Doc Cooper made himself heard above the tumult. "But what the devil was Baxter doing in that tunnel?" he demanded. The talk stilled to catch Berry's reply.

"I don't know," Berry said, "but I figure maybe he trailed a couple of prowlers to the tunnel and maybe lost 'em in the dark. Reckon he 'lowed they must have gone into the tunnel and planned to go in after them and catch 'em dead to rights. I don't know, but that might have been it."

"But how come his body was found half a mile up the valley?" the coroner asked.

Berry fumbled his hat in nervous hands, looked miserable. "Doc," he said slowly, "we packed him up there. When we found out who the deadfall had squashed we were almighty scared and didn't know what to do. Bayles 'lowed that when folks found out what we'd done they'd lynch us. Courtney said even if they didn't, a jury would find us guilty of murder and the judge would have us hanged. I didn't know what to think, but I was plumb scared, too. So we talked it over and decided the best thing to do was haul him out of the tunnel and put him somewhere so it'd look like he tumbled off the cliff and got killed by accident. We did just that and took his horse up top the cliffs to make it look better. I tell you we were scared and didn't know what else to do. But just the same I didn't feel right. I couldn't sleep. I'd keep seeing him how he looked under those infernal rocks. I got up and brought our week's washing of nuggets to town, but when I got back I still couldn't sleep and I kept feeling worse. I didn't get a wink of sleep last night, either, and the boys were just as bad. We figured we'd have to do something or go plumb loco, so we decided the best thing was to come and tell the truth. And that's how it stands. If you figure to lock me up, I reckon I ain't got no kick coming, only don't do anything to Bayles and Courtney. It was me figured that infernal deadfall, they weren't to blame."

He sighed deeply, squared his shoulders again and waited expectantly.

The coroner's jury hastily conferred in low tones with much clucking and shaking of heads. Finally Doc Cooper stood up and announced the decision.

"Gents," he said, "what happened to poor old Clem was mighty, mighty bad, but I don't see how we can blame Russ Berry. He had a right to try and protect his property, even if he did figure out a loco way to do it. He certainly didn't intend to kill Baxter or any other honest jigger. So I reckon the verdict still stands that poor Clem met his death by accident. And Russ, the next time you get a bright notion, just forget it fast."

Berry mumbled a word of thanks and looked greatly relieved.

"Russ, you did right by coming in and telling the truth," Wes Hargrove said kindly. "Always best to tell the truth. Now you've got it off your mind you'll feel better. And now I suggest we all go over to the Dun Cow and have a drink. I figure we need one. Come on, Sam, come on, Slade."

Slade went. He felt that he really did need one. What had looked like a promising lead had abruptly blown up in his face. He did not doubt that what Berry said was just what had happened. His story rang true. Besides, he didn't credit Berry with enough brains to concoct any such yarn out of the whole cloth.

There was just one thread that still dangled mockingly from the disrupted pattern — what was Sheriff Baxter doing in that mine tunnel? Slade did not go along with Berry's theory that he had followed ore thieves into the tunnel. Ore thieves were daring and desperate men and would shoot to kill, knowing that they would get short shrift from the enraged miners if captured. There would be no trial, just a rope across the most convenient tree branch. Sheriff Baxter, a canny and experienced old peace officer, would have known that and would never have gone groping into a dark tunnel in the wake of such gentry. If he had reason to believe prowlers were in the tunnel, he would have waited outside and gotten the drop on them when they emerged.

Yes, Sheriff Baxter very likely had some other reason for entering the tunnel. Slade hadn't the slightest notion what it could have been, but the problem greatly intrigued him.

Crane Arnold sauntered up to where Slade and Yelverton were standing and greeted them cordially. He glanced toward where Russ Berry and his two partners were drinking together.

"Looks like that big troublemaker has a streak of decency in him after all," he observed. "I would have been of the opinion that he wouldn't have been in the least affected by what happened in his tunnel. To dispose of the body at the foot of that slope would have been right in line with his way of thinking, I would have said. Dispose of it and forget the whole business and be perfectly satisfied with the way things were working out, himself in the clear and everything. Would appear, however, that he has a conscience, which I certainly wouldn't have credited him with. Interesting, isn't it, how you can totally misjudge a person? Perhaps my judgment was biased, though. He's been an irritation to me, one way or another, ever since he started coming in here."

"It's difficult to refrain from thinking the worst of an individual when he continually rubs you the wrong way," Slade agreed.

"And in this business it's hard to keep from thinking ill of someone who has a tendency for making trouble," Arnold nodded. "We have enough of it as is, under normal circumstances. A fellow who always has a chip on his shoulder is a nuisance in any drinking establishment. I always try to remember, however, that it's the stuff I sell from my side of the bar that causes the trouble on the other side. If I only sold soda pop, there'd always be peace and quiet."

"Not necessarily with a jigger like Berry," Yelverton put in. "He did the right thing today, but it doesn't alter the fact that he's hot-tempered and always ready to get his bristles up. And as you say, that's an infernal nuisance in this kind of a place. I know. I ran this one for better'n five years before you took over. But you asked for it, and I was darn glad to get out from under."

Arnold chuckled and with a pleasant nod returned to his customary position behind the gold-weighing counter.

Old Sam was silent for some minutes, sipping his drink and studying his surroundings. Abruptly he turned to Slade. "Son," he said, "over there in the corner's a vacant table with nobody close around. Suppose we amble over there and sit down. I'd like to talk to you a mite."

Slade was agreeable. After they sat down, Yelverton ordered another drink, loaded his pipe and for a while regarded Slade through the blue mist of the smoke. Slade, who was in the habit of allowing the other man to start a conversation, also smoked in silence, his gaze constantly roving over the room which was filling up as evening drew near. Finally old Sam spoke.

"Son," he said, "Frank Nance has been a friend of mine for the past thirty years. He's close-mouthed but he told me, in strict confidence, what happened there the other night. Looks like you've got a pack of killers on your trail."

"Could be," Slade replied noncommittally.

"Oh, I suppose you're used to it," conceded Yelverton. "By the way, don't you happen to have another handle folks call you by at times? Something that means a hawk in Mexican talk?"

Slade let his gaze rest on the old fellow's face a moment. "I have been called El Halcon," he said and smiled.

Yelverton didn't appear surprised. "So I gathered," he said. "And by the way, I was talking with old Jim McNelty not long ago — he's another old friend of mine — and he sure spoke mighty high of a young feller who works for him. Couldn't seem to talk enough about him."

Slade's eyes were dancing with laughter. "A little short fellow with yellow hair and one eye?"

"That's right," old Sam replied, grave as a judge. "Yep, that's the feller. Jim said he usually goes disguised to look big and tall and have black hair and both eyes. Mighty clever at disguises, I gather. Reckon he needs to be in his business. I just mentioned him because I figure old Jim would feel mighty bad if anything happened to that young feller. He should keep his eyes skun if he happens to be in this section. There's mighty funny things and mighty bad things been going on hereabouts of late. I figure that feller ain't up against no ordinary brand of brush poppin' owlhoots. Somebody hereabouts has got brains and knows how to use 'em."

"I'm inclined to agree with you," Slade said soberly. "And I gather, sir, that you don't believe that Ben Sutler just fell over a cliff or something?"

"No, I don't think he did," Yelverton replied. "In fact, as I said the other night, I can't help but feel Ben is alive."

"Why?"

"Well, for a couple of reasons," Yelverton explained. "For one, his body was never found, although we went over the valley and the hills on each side of it mighty careful. For another, that ornery skewbald he always rode wasn't found either, not hide or hoof of him. That critter was one of the smartest horses I ever saw. He'd never have got caught under a rock fall or tumbled over a cliff, and he never would have left Ben, dead or alive. They both just sort of vanished."

"And you figure that if Ben Sutler really is dead, he was murdered."

Old Sam jumped a little. "I never said that," he protested.

"No, but you're thinking it," Slade said quietly. "As I understand, Sutler had a hidden claim somewhere, a very rich one, for which he might well have been murdered, and the claim was not in Jericho Valley."

"I guess you're right about that," Yelverton agreed. "Ben's claim wasn't in Jericho Valley, that I'm pretty sure of. In fact, I am sure. If it was there he couldn't possibly have kept it hidden. The valley isn't very wide and less than fifteen miles long altogether. Not more'n half that is being worked. Down to this end is where the gold-bearing gravel is. Six or seven miles farther up the gravel beds and shale banks peter out. Up there are just straight-up-and-down cliffs of hard rock."

"No way out of the valley up there?"

"Yes, there's a way out," Yelverton replied. "The valley ends at a long slope that ain't too steep for riding. Folks must have ridden it way back in the old days sometime, for there's what used to be a pretty well-traveled trail up the slope that leads along a hogback and finally gets down to level ground north of the ridge. A pretty good-sized crik, almost a river, down to the west of the ridge, but cliffs shut it in where the slope ends, not so high cliffs, forty to fifty feet, but sheer. It's swift and deep and washes the base of the cliffs."

Slade nodded. Doubtless the stream of which old Sam spoke was the river that originally ran down Jericho Valley and very likely carried a much larger volume of water before the vulcanic disturbances changed its course. Yelverton's description of the terrain sounded interesting and Slade decided to have a look at it soon.

That night there was a meeting of the county commissioners and after some debate, Chief Deputy Clifton Yates was appointed to fill out Sheriff Baxter's unexpired term of office.

"I sort of favored Tom Horrel," old Sam Yelverton confided to Slade. "He's a smart jigger and familiar with the sheriff's duties. But Crane Arnold attended the meeting and spoke up for Yates. Crane had done Wes Hargrove and Doc Beard quite a few favors and his recommendation carried weight with them. It was Arnold who got Baxter to appoint Yates chief deputy in the first place. I had nothing against Yates so I strung my vote along with theirs. He was all right and well-liked when he worked for Arnold, and he appears to be a hustler. Reckon he'll be okay once he gets the hang of things. If he is, he can get elected next time, if he decides to run."

Slade nodded but didn't otherwise comment. He was willing to concede that Clifton Yates' personality would win him popularity, but whether he possessed the qualifications necessary to the making of an efficient peace officer remained to be seen. However, Yates was new on the job and readily admitted that he had a lot to learn, which was to his credit. Perhaps he would make out all right. Anyhow he appeared to be energetic and ambitious.

Old Sam contemplated the growing crowd. "Some folks say I was a darn fool to sell out like I did," he observed reflectively. "They say I gave away a bigger gold mine than any in Jericho Valley."

"You didn't," Slade said shortly.

Old Sam stared at him. "What do you mean, son?" he asked.

"I mean," Slade replied, "that this time next year Sotol will be a sleepy cowtown just like it was before the strike in Jericho Valley. Long before that the gold in Jericho Valley will have petered out."

"But, son, Crane Arnold and Russ Berry, who claim to know plenty about mining, say the Jericho Valley mines are practically inexhaustible," Yelverton protested. "They say the shale banks run clean up to the rimrock and that the deeper you go the richer the gold deposits will get."

"Well, if they say that, they claim a familiarity with mining they certainly don't possess," Slade observed drily. "Here's how the situation stands."

Briefly he described to Yelverton the geological formation of the valley and its significance. Yelverton shook his head in bewilderment.

"The way you put it, you sure sound like you know what you're talking about," he admitted. "But how about the gold Ben Sutler brought in? It's pretty well-established that he never mined that gold in Jericho Valley, but he sure brought in plenty and he must have got it somewhere."

"That has me puzzled," Slade admitted. "Is there another valley similar to Jericho in the Ashes Mountains?"

"Man and boy I've lived here for better'n seventy years and I never heard of one," Yelverton replied. "I figure I can say for sure there ain't. I was all through those dusty chunks back in the old days and I sure never saw one."

"Then," Slade said with finality, "if Sutler didn't get his gold from Jericho Valley, he didn't dig it anywhere in the Ashes Mountains. There isn't a gold-bearing ledge in those lava formations. The gold in Jericho Valley is strictly alluvial gold and will be found only in the gravel that bases the lower shale banks which were once under water.

Farther up the slopes there will be nothing. It looks like Sutler must have had his hidden mine somewhere way up in the Guadalupes, which poses a question. As I understand, there were times when he would be absent for only a few days and then would come in with a filled poke."

"That's right," said Yelverton. "He did it lots of times."

"Then I'm darned if I know where he got it," Slade admitted. "Perhaps he did have a hidden mine somewhere in Jericho Valley."

Yelverton shook his head positively. "Just wouldn't have been possible," he declared. "Whenever Ben slipped out of town, the valley was full of gents trying to learn where he had his diggin'. If he'd had it in the valley they'd have spotted him sure."

"Then apparently there's no answer to the question," Slade said thoughtfully. "That is none anybody has managed to hit on so far. Interesting."

"Darn interesting," nodded Yelverton, "and I've a notion the answer to it will tie up with what happened to poor Ben."

"I think you're safe in assuming that," Slade agreed.

Chapter Nine

The following day Walt Slade rode into Jericho Valley. Just what he expected to find there he was not himself sure, but he was curious about the place and wanted to examine the unusual formation more closely. He rode at a slow pace, his eyes roving over the frowning cliffs and the precipitous slopes. At the mouth of the valley and for quite some disstance within it there was nothing but an air of arid desolation, but before long the dreary monotony gave way to a scene of cheerful and bustling activity. He began passing shacks and leantos, and men busily burrowing into the shale banks or washing gravel in the creek. Many of them called a greeting, but some were too busy to even glance up as he rode past.

And yet, death in various forms was always present. More than once a warning buzz sounded from the growth that flanked the trail on the west, causing Shadow to snort nervously, and several times Slade saw big snakes stretched out on rocks for the brief sunning the rattler can endure. Undoubtedly the gorge was alive with the legless devils. There must be a large den of the reptiles somewhere in the canyon, Slade reflected, knowing that rattlesnakes live in a gregarious fashion during the cold weather, holing up in caves or other subterranean sanctuaries.

Several times, also, he noted springs of white and still water, with an ominous frosting on the stones that indicated arsenic. And once a rock fall thundered down somewhere ahead. Only the lure of gold could bring men into such an inferno of heat, dust and danger. But because of the yellow metal they were here, pitting their lives against the hazards of malevolent nature in their lust for gain.

Finally Slade reached Russ Berry's cabin, some miles up the valley. Nobody was about so he rode on till he approached the mine tunnel where Sheriff Baxter met an untimely end. Berry and his two companions, Bayles and Courtney, were busily washing gravel in the stream that ran past the tunnel mouth to curve around a bristle of chaparral and disappear from sight.

Berry straightened up and waved a greeting. "Hard work, feller," he called, "but it pays better'n following a cow's tail. Unfork and have a look."

Slade dismounted and strolled to the creek bank. With a jerk of his thumb, Berry indicated a small heap of dull-colored lumps on a blanket.

"There she is," he said. "Help yourself to one for a souvenir. Make a nice watch charm."

Slade accepted the invitation and squatted beside the heap. He turned the nuggets over in his fingers and finally selected a small one of symmetrical shape.

"Heck, take a big one," invited Berry. "That one's just piddlin'. Go ahead, plenty more in that hole where these came from. We won't miss it."

"This one is just right for what I have in mind," Slade replied. "A bigger one would be too heavy. Thanks a lot."

Berry wiped his muddy hand on his overalls, fished out the makin's and began rolling a cigarette cowboy fashion with one hand. Courtney and Bayles paused from their work to follow his example.

"Aim to maybe stake a claim?" Berry asked when he had gotten the brain tablet going good. "About all the worthwhile ground here to the east has been tied onto, but I've a notion there ought to be something over to the west. Nobody has staked over there, but I don't see any reason why there shouldn't be metal in those rocks, too."

"I may take a whirl at it," Slade admitted. "I think I'll ride on to the head of the valley and look things over. Might be something good in the creek up there, never can tell."

"That's right," nodded Berry. "Well, good hunting!"

Slade mounted and rode on. As soon as he was out of sight around a bend, Berry turned to his companions.

"All right, you jiggers," he said. "You claim to be the best brushcombers in the state, and I'll admit you've proved yourselves purty good. See what you can do. But get him between you — don't bunch together. He's bad and he's smart, as you had a little example a while back. Don't take any chances with the hellion. Remember, don't cut loose at him till you get him between you, and don't get close."

"You think maybe he's caught onto something, Russ?" Courtney asked nervously as he stepped from the water.

"Don't think he has, yet," Berry answered, "but I've a notion he's suspicious. You know his reputation for ferreting things out. If he's allowed to keep snooping around he might catch onto something, and we can't afford that. Can't anybody tell me he just came up here for the ride. He's got some kind of a notion in his mind. Anyhow, we won't take any chances. Go ahead and get rid of him. It's your chore, and see you don't bungle it."

Courtney hesitated. "Russ," he objected, "the valley to the north of here is open, mighty little brush, and that hellion's got sharp eyes and is a devil of a good shot. Ain't good dry-gulching country up there."

Berry pondered a moment. "Tell you what," he said at length, "we'll do a little gambling on him. I'm sure as blazes he's up here hunting for something. Mighty unlikely he'll find anything to interest him in the valley north of here, and what he'll see won't look promising. But if he really figures there's something worth looking for, I'm willing to bet that when he sees the trail climbing the sag to the north he'll be curious enough about where it leads to follow it, for a while, anyhow. So cut way around to the west and get ahead of him. He won't spot your riding along the west wall — too far. Once you get him up over the lip of the sag you should be able to close in on him without taking too big a chance. And anyhow orders are orders and you know what happens to folks who don't obey 'em."

He fixed them with a hard stare as he spoke. Bayles and Courtney looked uncomfortable.

"Okay! okay!" said the latter. "They way you figure it sounds like a good notion. Come on, Chuck, we'll handle it that way."

He and Bayles left the creek bank and hurried to the cabin. A little later they rode west across the valley and then turned north.

As he rode slowly up the canyon, Slade drew from his pocket the nugget Berry had given him and studied it long and earnestly, shaking his head, the concentration furrow deep between his black brows. Finally he engaged Shadow in an argument over it.

"I don't care what you say, horse, this thing was not dug from that tunnel," he declared. "It's alluvial gold, all right, but it has been exposed to the air and light for many, many years. The color and surface indications prove that, definitely. And the same goes for every nugget in that heap. Now what's the answer? This business grows more puzzling by the minute."

Shadow snorted general disagreement and declined to discuss the matter further. Slade continued to turn the problem over in his mind. He was convinced of one thing. In some manner the mystery tied up with the death of Sheriff Baxter, but why and how? What did the sheriff expect to find in that tunnel? It appeared that he had obtained some information he thought worthy of investigating. Something to do with the activities of Russ Berry and his companions? It was logical to believe so.

This brought him back to the lump of gold that baffled explanation. Was Berry engaged in some ingenious "salting" scheme? It was not beyond the realm of possibility that he was salting a worthless claim, with gold he smuggled in and mixed with the gravel in the tunnel, with the intention of selling the apparently valuable holding to somebody for a big price. Such things had been done, many times. Wade Buchanan, the great actor, bought a commanding interest in a Nevada silver mine that produced metal of marvellous richness, and paid a tremendous price for the holding. Later it came to light that the claim had been salted in an outrageously brazen manner. Salted with melted silver half-dollars! Berry might be working up to a similar swindle. Maybe Sheriff Baxter had caught onto what he had in mind and had been out to get proof of

Berry's crookedness.

He thought of the gold stolen from the wagon wrecked in the canyon. A good way to get the nuggets into circulation — slip them into the tunnel, mix them with the gravel and then "honestly" wash them out. Could Berry have had a hand in the robbery?

However, he immediately discarded the idea. The gold stolen from the wagon had been mined from the shale banks of Jericho Valley, no doubt about that. Its color and surface condition proved it beyond a doubt. The nugget he held in his hand had not been mined from the shale banks, at least at no time in the immediate past. With a mutter of disgust, Slade gave up for the time being and turned his attention to the terrain over which he was riding. Soon he passed the last staked claim and quickly saw why it was the last.

The nature of the valley had changed. The long shale banks were no longer in evidence and had been replaced by tall cliffs of dark stone. They were curiously striated, in a manner which is characteristic of basaltic upheavals, as Slade well knew. Their summit showed signs of fairly luxuriant vegetation, with bushes near the edge and trees farther back. On the valley floor, growth was contrastingly sparse, for the soil was stony. In fact, from various indications Slade concluded that here the ancient river had run in a wide-bottomed trough of rock, which accounted for the fact that the gold had been deposited nearer the mouth of the gorge. He saw no more arsenic springs.

One disagreeable phenomenon of the valley had not changed, however. The snakes were just as plentiful as lower down the gorge; more so, in fact. Slade counted a full dozen of the varmints in the course of a mile. Keeping a watchful eye out for chance squirms that might have invaded the track, he quickened Shadow's pace and rode on until he perceived the slope which boxed the valley on the north. When he reached it he discovered that the stream, whose course he had been paralleling, poured from an opening in the base of the slope. Quite likely it was the residue of the river that once flowed down the valley, achieving entrance to the gorge by way of a subterranean channel. And winding up the long, brush-grown slope, the trail continued on its way.

At the base of the slope, Slade pulled Shadow to a halt, fished out his tobacco and papers and rolled a cigarette. Hooking one long leg comfortably over the horn he sat smoking and studying the vista ahead.

North of the shale banks he had noted nothing of significance. The cliffs walling the valley on the east were absolutely sheer — a lizard would have to double-head to get up them — and to all appearances those to the west were a similar formation. Anybody going north through the valley with some objective in mind would have to leave the gorge by way of the north slope. It was logical to believe that it indicated old Ben Sutler had followed it to reach his hidden claim. And Slade had a convincing hunch that in some way Sutler's gold was tied with the mystery of who was plaguing the section with lawless acts. He decided to follow the trail for a while and see where it led. Pinching out the butt, he sent Shadow up the winding track.

When he reached the crest, the hogback of which Yelverton had spoken lay before him, stretching into the north for as far as the eye could reach. It was a narrow spine of naked stone but level and comparatively smooth, offering easy passage for a mounted man.

To the east the slope was impossible to negotiate, consisting of broken stone, huge boulders and benches with precipitous sides. The west was different. The slope was gentle, dropping down by easy stages to the distant rim of the cliffs that flanked the river below. It was devoid of growth for about six hundred yards down the sag from where Slade sat his horse. Then a belt of dense chaparral began, clothing the soil with its bristling tangle to the cliff edge. About a quarter of a mile ahead the terrain was again different, being sparsely grown with bushes and a few trees. This condition obtained for something like five hundred yards, when again the heavy growth took over and continued on into the distance.

Riding up the northern stretch of Jericho Valley, Slade had paid little attention to other than his immediate surroundings and the cliff walls which hemmed the valley in. From wall to wall was open ground. But now he abruptly became very much on the alert. Riding the hogback, outlined against the sky, he now afforded an excellent target. It was comforting to note that the growth which would provide cover for anybody with notions was hundreds of yards distant. Not too far, however, for a good marksman to score a hit in a few tries.

He rode slowly, passing the first distant belt of chaparral and arriving at the edge of the stretch of sparsely-covered ground. Ahead, now less than five hundred yards, the second belt began, a dense bristle, the leaves and twigs catching the sunlight that was slanting from the west. Slade regarded the tangled chaparral with interest and a slightly disquieting feeling. With less to fear from the cover behind, he concentrated on that ahead, searching the dark stand with a gaze that missed nothing, slowing Shadow's gait more and more. And it was well he did.

As it was, he saw the puff of whitish smoke mushroom up from the brush now about four hundred yards to the front. Instantly he hurled himself down onto Shadow's neck, wheeling him "on a dime" and sending him charging down the thinly-brushed slope. The slug yelled overhead before he heard the whiplash crack of the report.

"Trail, Shadow," he shouted and sent the black charging for a clump of brush a hundred yards or so distant.

Another bullet whined past, and another, close. Slade felt the wind of the next one and breathed a sigh of relief as he flashed behind the sheltering bush. And then, just as he was pulling up and reaching for his Winchester in the saddle boot, another slug screeched past. And this one came from the belt of chaparral to the south!

Walt Slade began to think very hard indeed. He had blundered into a trap and was caught between a deadly cross-fire. His present position was untenable. Sheltered from the marksman to the north, he was a prime target for the one to the south, and he could see nothing to shoot at. Again he sent Shadow scudding down the slope. It was imperative that he keep moving and provide as elusive a target as possible until he found some place to hole up.

The bullets kept coming, whining overhead, or kicking up spurts of dust from the ground, ricocheting from stones. Shadow squealed with pain and anger as one flicked a patch of hide from his glossy haunch. Another ripped a hole through the crown of Slade's hat. The devils could shoot and they knew their business. They were paralleling him in the shadow of the sheltering growth, and they were getting the range. Ahead were more clumps of brush, but none large enough to provide effectual concealment. If he paused in one, the drygulchers would only have to concentrate their fire on it, knowing that sooner or later a slug would find its mark. The best he could do was zigzag between the sparse stands, hidden for a moment from one rifleman but plainly in sight to the other. And he was steadily drawing nearer the cliff rim and a sheer drop through nothingness from a height that would be fatal to man and horse. Looked like the only thing he could do was dismount, hug the ground and hope to take a least one of the hellions with him; and the odds were all against even that.

Nearer and nearer drew the cliff edge, with the clusters of brush growing smaller and with greater space between them. Directly ahead was the jagged rimrock and to all appearances the end of the trail. Only his mount's erratic movements had saved him so far, but he couldn't keep moving forever. The drygulchers could really shoot and once he came to a halt and provided them with a stationary mark they wouldn't miss. Yes, this was it! A funny way to end it all, but here it was — trail's end!

Only forty yards more to go. To his ears came the roar of swift water rising from the depths. The cliff edge was naked stone that provided no possible shelter. And still the slugs whined past. Slade felt that it was a miracle that one hadn't gone home before now. He strained his eyes toward the distant chaparral belt, hoping to catch a glimpse of one of the devils, but only the traveling puffs of smoke showed white for an instant against the dark background. Ten yards to go — sixty feet and ten seconds of life!

And then through his mind flashed the words of old Sam Yelverton — *"It's swift and deep and washes the base of the cliffs!"* And he had said the cliffs were only forty or fifty feet high. A chance! A last mad gamble with death. If there were rocks beneath . . .

Slade didn't hesitate. His voice rang out, urgent, compelling, "Trail, Shadow, trail! Take it, feller, take it!"

Instantly the great horse shot forward, blowing and snorting, his irons ringing on the stones. The broken lip rushed toward them. The thunder of angry water rose above the drumming of the flying hoofs. Shadow squealed with fright, faltered an instant.

"Take it!" Slade roared.

Chapter Ten

Shadow took it, with an almost human scream of terror. Over the lip of the cliff he soared. Slade had a fleeting glimpse of dark fangs of stone rising like living things from a waste of white water. And then they struck, with a surging plunge, grazing a spire of naked rock. Slade flung himself from the saddle as they went down and down into the icy depths. With one hand he gripped the bit iron, with the other the pommel of the saddle as the frantic horse struggled with all his great strength to rise.

It seemed to Slade that they were under water for many minutes, although reason told him it was only a few seconds. His lungs were bursting when they at last broke surface together and were caught by the full force of the current and instantly submerged again. But in that instant horse and man had filled their lungs full of life-giving air.

This time they were under water but a

moment, rising to the surface with the push of the current behind them. Slade could see the cliff face flickering past. The little river ran like a mill race. Fighting to keep Shadow's head up, stroking desperately with his legs, he glanced ahead. Less than a fifth of a mile away the stream frothed around a bulge. But on the rimrock above appeared the shape of a mounted man. He swung to the ground, ran forward and paused, rifle raised.

Slade saw the puff of smoke, heard the spat of the bullet on the water a few yards off. Another puff and another slapping sound, closer this time. He went under, dragging the snorting horse with him, fighting to keep them both submerged as long as possible. Unable to endure the torture any longer he broke surface, and again heard the ominous spat of the ricocheting slug.

But now the thin crack of the rifle came from behind, and nearer and nearer loomed the cliff bulge around which the river swept.

A last angry whine of lead passed so close its lethal break fanned his face. To Slade's whirling brain that quick whine seemed to hold a baffled note as the current flung them around the bulge and safe from further bullets.

But Slade soon wondered if he had simply traded a swift death on the land for a slower but nonetheless sure one in the water. Its icy bite and the fierce pounding of the current numbed his muscles and sapped his strength. And to make matters worse, the drive of the current was toward the cliff wall, the stream raving and foaming against that seamless barrier and flinging back in dizzy whirlpools.

Even Shadow's iron might was failing and it was all Slade could do to prevent him from succumbing to utter panic and fatal struggling. All they could do was breast the current sufficiently to keep from being pounded to a pulp against the cliffs.

Suddenly a fresh terror made itself heard, a low thundering that could mean but one thing; no great distance ahead the river surged over a fall of great height. Once again Slade was ready to give himself up for lost. They could never hope to survive the plunge into the frothing catch basin with tons of water crushing them down against the rocks. His eyes half blinded by fatigue and the dashing spray, he craned his head up to peer ahead.

Yes, there it was, less than two hundred yards distant, the smooth, curving lip of the cataract. The sight of that snakelike ripple of death revived him for one last frantic effort. Gripping Shadow's bit iron, he let go the pommel, flung his body around, dragging the home's head with him, and stroked madly with his legs and his free arm.

"Trail, feller, trail!" he croaked and gasped. "Take it, feller, trail!"

Under the inspiration of that rallying call, Shadow made a final gallant effort. His irons spurned the roiling water even as they had so often spurned the surface of the trail. He lunged forward, snorting and blowing, with Slade fighting the current beside him and panting encouragement.

With agonizing slowness they forged away from the beetling wall that raced past so swiftly and toward the stretch of pebbly beach which flanked the stream on the west. The loudening thunder of the fall dinned in their ears. The accelerating current ripped and tore at them. An upthrust of black stone with cruel jagged edges loomed before them. They grazed it, and what had threatened destruction proved their salvation. The obstacle swerved the current and formed an eddy that whirled them from the middle of the stream toward the shelving west bank. Another moment of despairing struggle, with the serpentine lip of the fall reaching its coils hungrily toward them, and Shadow's irons clashed on the rocky bottom. Half swimming, half wading, horse and man floundered through the shallows to the beach and safety.

For long minutes, Slade lay prone on the sun-warmed pebbles, retching and gasping. Shadow stood beside him, legs widespread, his head hanging as he breathed in sobbing pants.

Finally Slade sat up and grinned wanly at the horse. "Well, feller, we made it, which was more than I hoped for at one time," he said.

Shadow rolled a gleaming, though slightly watery, eye and appeared too disgusted with things in general to voice a comment. Slade chuckled and proceeded to take stock of his surroundings. Beyond the pebbly strand grass grew and a little farther on were bristles of thicket. He eyed them with satisfaction. It was warm on the little beach but a glance at the low lying sun told him that soon there would be a chill in the air and his drenched clothes would become uncomfortable. He managed to drag off his soaked boots and empty them of water. Next he made sure his guns were in working order.

These matters attended to, he examined

the contents of his saddle pouches. They were intact, though a trifle damp. Coffee and some flour in rubber pouches had been little affected and water doesn't hurt bacon. And half a dozen eggs, carefully wrapped, had miraculously escaped breakage. His tightly-corked flat bottle of matches was also undamaged.

The sight of the food reminded him that he was ravenously hungry. Well, there was just one thing to do about that and he decided to do it. Shadow had recovered enough to begin to show interest in the grass that clothed the prairie beyond the river bank. Slade forked him and rode to one of the nearer thickets, a sizeable patch of tall brush past which a trickle of water flowed to join the river. He eyed the close bristle with favor. Here was plenty of dry wood. He dismounted, got the rig off Shadow and turned him loose to graze.

"Go to it, you old grassburner," he told the horse. "I think I can risk lighting a fire. Don't think those hellions can get down to the level ground unless they care to risk a dive through nothing at a herd of rocks, which I don't think they do. Anyhow, it's very likely they figured we were sure to drown. In fact, I think some gents will be quite surprised when we show up in town," he added grimly.

With Shadow cared for, Slade quickly got a fire going. Soon bacon and eggs were sizzling in a small skillet, coffee steaming in a little flat bucket. Slade's clothes were also steaming in the heat. His tobacco and papers were spread on a warmed rock to dry. The fire transmuted flour, water and bacon grease into a succulent doughcake to round out an appetizing meal.

Full fed and content, Slade stretched out on his blanket and smoked in peaceful relaxation. With the resilience of youth and perfect health he had thrown off the effects of his recent harrowing experience and was dreamily satisfied with the present. The sun had set and the lovely blue dusk was sifting down from the hilltops like impalpable dust. Overhead, the bonfire stars of Texas began to blaze in splendor, their light touching the grassheads with pale silver. Through the soft hush floated the murmur of the river, sounding quite different to his ears than had its hungry growl when he battled it for his life. All in all, he had no complaint with the way things had worked out.

For a while he let his mind idle along meandering paths of physical well being and creature comfort, but gradually he settled down to some serious thinking. He thought about this second attempt on his life to have occurred in the space of a few days. Somebody was grimly tenacious of purpose. Who, and why? The obvious answer to both questions was that the gold-wagon robbers were out to avenge the killing of one of their number, but the answer was not altogether satisfactory. There were a few salient points that needed clearing up. The first try, the one in the hotel room, hinted at an angry and impulsive reprisal. But the second denoted careful planning and, on the surface, at least, an almost clairvoyant anticipation of his movements. It was not beyond the realm of probability the bunch had been keeping a close watch on him, had seen him ride into Jericho Valley and had decided that the desolate gorge was ideal for a drygulching. But that they should deliberately ride on ahead and wait for him beyond the limits of the gorge presumed a remarkably correct interpretation of his reason for entering the valley. Which he felt predicated something not so transparent as the revenge motive.

Was there something in the valley or its environs that somebody was desperately anxious he should not discover? Slade was inclined to think that was the more logical assumption. What? He didn't have the answer. But that and another question kept drawing together as parallel lines seem to in the distance. What did Sheriff Clem Baxter hope to find in Russ Berry's mine tunnel? Although he had absolutely nothing tangible upon which to base the supposition, Slade felt that if he had the answer to the one, he had the answer to the other.

It was inevitable that his train of thought should curve around till it focused on the heap of nuggets Russ Berry intimated he dug from his claim in the shale bank, but which Slade was convinced had not, at any recent date, been gleaned from Jericho Valley's alluvial deposit. Berry had lied by insinuation. Following the argument to its logical conclusion, it must infer that Berry had something to conceal. Did Sheriff Baxter definitely suspect what that elusive something was, endeavor to find out for sure and find his death instead? Slade believed so.

All of which he was force to admit was in the nature of an argument with himself, an endeavor to prove or disprove his personal conviction that Russ Berry and his two companions were responsible for the recent attack. A careful analysis of the situation did point the finger of suspicion at Berry, although in honesty Slade had to concede that his analysis might well be faulty. And if it was not, it hinted at a cleverness and a subtle mental equipment with which he would never have credited the burly miner. In fact, despite the accumulation of indirect evidence, he was still hesitant to endow Berry with such attributes.

All in all, an excellent example of hindsight versus foresight, he concluded in a mood for self-censure. A little careful deduction in advance might have saved him an abominable experience and some agonizing moments during which he thought that his number was up.

Comforted by what amounted to honest confession, he fell to sleep.

CHAPTER ELEVEN

Slade was astir with the first light. He cooked a somewhat scanty breakfast from his remaining provisions, gave Shadow a good rubdown and got the rig on him. Before setting out on his search for a way back to town, he rode to where the river plunged into its sunken gorge.

He shivered a little as he gazed into the shadowy depths where the falling water foamed and thundered. If they had gone over that the day before, man and horse would have instantly been pounded to a plup.

"But we didn't," he told Shadow cheerfully, "so there's no use bothering our heads about what might have happened. June along, horse, we got places to go and have to figure a way to get there."

Slade hadn't the slightest notion where he was, but he knew that Sotol must lie somewhere to the east. However, he was forced to ride many miles before the gorge petered out and he could ford the river, now broad and shallow. But he had been riding south and when he finally hit a trail he had no great distance to go, reaching the cowtown about mid-afternoon. He stabled Shadow, crossed to the roominghouse and ascended to his room. Thankfully he donned a clean shirt and overalls and oiled and polished his boots till he got the stiffness out of them. Then he gave attention to his guns. His hat, which the chin strap had held in place during his battle with the river, was somewhat of a mess, but a little slapping and pounding and shaping made it fairly presentable. With these matters attended to, he headed for the Dun Cow and something to eat.

When he entered the saloon he found old Sam Yelverton at the bar and paused to have a drink with him.

"Where were you last night?" Yelverton asked. "Missed you."

"I took a little ride," Slade replied carelessly. "Anything exciting?"

"Nothing much except Russ Berry and his two partners sort of went on a toot," Yelverton answered. "They did considerable swallerforking all evening. Russ said they'd hit a extra rich pocket and figured a little celebration was in order."

Slade reflected grimly that if his surmise was correct, Berry and his pals would be in a less jovial mood on the morrow. He had a pretty fair notion as to just what the celebration was about. The way things worked out, it had been a bit premature.

"Crane Arnold is a bit more tolerant of that big hellion since he came clean about what happened to poor Clem Baxter," Yelverton remarked reminiscently. "He just grinned at their shenanigans last night. Sheriff Yates came in, watched them a minute or two, chuckled and went out. Berry better not be playing his luck too strong, though. Folks feel sort of kind toward him right now, but he can spoil that in a hurry if he starts raising the devil again. He didn't know it, maybe, but he was asking to have a vigilance committee pay him a visit and suggest some other locality might be a bit healthier. There's a limit how much of a darn nuisance a feller can make of himself in even a tough town like Sotol."

A few minutes later Sheriff Clifton Yates came in. Slade was conversing with Yelverton and didn't notice his entrance until he approached the bar.

The new sheriff's handsome face wore a strained expression, Slade thought, and he looked like a man who had just received something of a shock. He immediately confirmed that he had.

"Gents," he said as he reached for his glass, "I'm beginning to find out this sheriffin' business ain't all peaches and cream. Ever since I was a kid I'd had a hankering to be a chief of police or a sheriff, but now I am one, I'm beginning to almost wish I wasn't."

"What's on your mind, Cliff?" Yelverton asked. "Having trouble?"

Yates nodded soberly. "I am," he said. "A little bit ago some fellers brought in the body of a poor devil of a miner they picked up in the mouth of Jericho Valley. Been shot in the back of the head. His poke gone, of course. Those fellers didn't talk nice to me. They said I was supposed to keep such things from happening, and if they managed to catch up with the son of a hydrophobia skunk who did it they weren't coming to the law, that there'd be a hanging first off and that quite a few hangings were in order, the way things have been going of late."

He paused, emptied half his glass. "One said it might be a good notion to start with the sheriff," he added.

Old Sam chuckled. Yates grinned wanly and emptied his glass. "Reckon I might as well ride up there and see if I can learn anything," he said and left the saloon.

Old Sam watched him out of sight, contemplatively, then turned to Slade. "What do you think of him?" he asked.

Slade shrugged his broad shoulders. "Hard to tell," he admitted. "As he said, a cowhand with an ambition to become a law-enforcement officer. Due to an unfortunate accident, he all of a sudden became one. Chances are he's still a bit bewildered and is beginning to realize that there's more to being the sheriff of a big county than wearing a badge and looking important. He's young, though. Perhaps he'll improve with age."

Old Sam looked dubious but did not argue the point. "Let's go eat," he suggested.

Slade spent the afternoon wandering about Sotol in Yelverton's company, meeting various town folks who greeted him cordially. Later there was a session of poker with old Sam and some of his cronies, the game breaking up around midnight.

It was shortly after midnight that Russ Berry came in. He nodded to Slade and Yelverton and walked to the gold-weighing counter. Slade studied him closely as he passed and was forced to admit that if Berry had anything to do with the attempted drygulching the day before he was an excellent actor. His countenance was impassive and he certainly didn't have the look expected of one who had celebrated a man's murder the night before and then suddenly came face to face with him in the flesh.

Berry passed a poke to Arnold. The saloonkeeper adjusted his scales and dumped the poke's contents in the pan. The metal lumps had a softly yellow look and glowed dully in the lamplight. Without doubt they were alluvial gold and had been but recently dug from the earth. They were quite different in appearance from the specimen Slade had in his pocket. So it would appear that Berry was digging gold from his claim. Perhaps his jamboree of the night before had been to celebrate the striking of an unusually rich pocket of the precious metal. But where did he get the weathered nuggets Slade watched him wash from the heap of gravel on the creek's bank? Slade had to admit that he was utterly baffled. Berry consistently refused to properly fit into the picture. Over and over he appeared in a light that was the antithesis of what Slade expected. He had analyzed Berry as an impulsive, belligerent and slightly stupid individual, but he was rapidly becoming very much of an enigma. Slade wondered just what new metamorphosis was to be expected of him.

Berry had a drink, conversed with Crane Arnold for a while and walked out. A few minutes after his departure Sheriff Yates came in and also talked with Arnold. Slade wondered if they were discussing Russ Berry and his antics and thought that very likely they were. Shortly afterward he went to bed in a disgusted frame of mind. It seemed that every time he had something building up, something happened to knock it down again.

The inquest held on the murdered miner's body followed a drearily monotonous pattern, the verdict being that he had met his death at the hands of a party or parties unknown. Added was a caustic condemnation of the sheriff's office and a recommendation that the sheriff hire some deputies who would know their business and do something to improve existing conditions. Sheriff Yates tugged his mustache, swore and looked badly worried.

"Up in the valley yesterday I didn't learn a thing," he confided to Yelverton, Doc Beard and Wes Hargrove, the big cattleman. "The boys are in a mighty bad temper. They say there's too darn many owlhoots drifting in of late and that something's got to be done about it."

Yates glanced keenly at Slade as he spoke. The Ranger repressed a smile. He wondered if somebody had quietly informed the sheriff that the "notorious" El Halcon was squatting in his bailwick. But if Yates had received any such information he kept it to himself.

"Son, I hope you're right about that infernal gold strike," old Sam observed to Slade as they left the sheriff's office together. "There won't be any peace hereabouts so long as metal keeps coming out of the valley." He paused, then added reflectively, "I was sort of sounding out Crane Arnold the other night. Didn't tell him what you told me, of course, just asked him if they thought the valley would go on producing gold. He said he was sure of it, that in his opinion the strike would last indefinitely, just as he said the other time I talked to him about it."

"I believe you said Arnold claimed to have had some mining experience," Slade remarked.

"Oh, he had it, all right," Yelverton replied. "I know some fellers who knew him over in California. They said he had a claim up around Placerville, the pueblo they used to call Hangtown. They said he dug quite a bit of metal but that the claim petered out, as it seems they have a habit of doing over there, and he went to work in a Placerville saloon. That's where he got started dealing cards, I reckon, though he may have been a dealer before he took up prospecting, I don't know."

"I see," Slade said thoughtfully. In fact, he was suddenly a bit puzzled about Crane Arnold, although not seriously so. The ravines around Placerville, originally known as Ravine City, from which the Placerville gold was drawn were of a formation similar to that of Jericho Valley, something any miner who had worked them would immediately recognize.

Of course there was an obvious explanation as to why Arnold did not see fit to divulge the knowledge he must have. Despite his affability, Slade had already catalogued Arnold as a cold proposition at the bottom. The gambling fraternity was made up of individuals who usually entertained few scruples when it came to dealings with their fellow men. Arnold, recognizing the Jericho Valley conditions for what they were, was very likely just waiting for the proper time to unload. The Dun Cow was a profitable business, as everybody knew. When Arnold decided that the Jericho Valley strike was about exhausted, no doubt he would announce his intention of moving elsewhere and put up his business for sale, knowing that he could expect an excellent price for what was to all appearances an exceedingly good investment. Yes, no doubt that was it.

His conclusion didn't tend to raise Arnold in Slade's estimation, but the coterie to which Arnold belonged would not see anything particularly off-color in such a transaction. If the sucker can't look out for himself, why should we look out for him? That was their philosophy and although others might regard it as false logic they lived by it and felt they were justified in doing so. With that fact in mind, Slade dismissed the matter with a shrug. Arnold was a gambler and would run his course to the end appointed for such as he. Slade resolved to eventually tangle *Señor* Arnold's twine for him in regard to his little scheme, but not yet. He had more important things to think about at the moment.

Slade and Yelverton had dinner together in the Dun Cow. Crane Arnold sauntered over with a word of greeting. He turned suddenly toward the bar as someone called to him and for the third time Slade experienced the conviction that he had recently encountered someone whose face greatly resembled that of the saloonkeeper, especially in profile. But the where or who still eluded him.

"I heard that poor feller who was killed had a nice fat poke on him," Yelverton remarked. "Crane Arnold handled his shipping and Crane said he hadn't been in for a couple of weeks and he figured he must have had plenty. Funny how the hellions seem to always know just where to hit to make a prime killing. Begins to look like they have a mighty smooth working organization."

Slade had arrived at that conclusion some time before and the robbers undoubtedly had access to some very reliable source of information. The gold-wagon robbery attested to that.

That night Russ Berry again put in an appearance, and again he brought along a poke of gold. Slade watched the weighing with interest.

Suddenly he leaned forward a little, his eyes narrowing. Unlike those of the night before, the dull-colored lumps gave off no softly aureate shimmer. They were weathered gold, long exposed to the elements, similar to the nugget Russ Berry gave him for a souvenir.

Slade raised his glance to Crane Arnold's face. It was expressionless as he adjusted the delicate balance. Surely he must have noticed this difference. Perhaps he did but reasoned that it was no affair of his. In which, of course, he was justified.

The question uppermost in Slade's mind was, where the devil did Berry get the stuff he palmed off as having been dug from his claim? It was a puzzler, but Slade was more than ever convinced that in some way it was the key to the mystery he was trying to solve, and very likely also the key to the mystery of old Ben Sutler's unexplained disappearance. He abruptly resolved to get a look into Berry's mine tunnel, fraught with danger though the attempt very probably would be.

Once again he wondered just why Sheriff Clem Baxter had entered the tunnel. He firmly believed that Baxter had learned something and was endeavoring to put it to the test. But what? Slade didn't have the answer to that one and wished he did.

Chapter Twelve

Slade spent the following day loafing around Sotol. He retired to his room early, but he didn't stay there. A couple of hours before midnight he got the rig on Shadow, slipped him out of the stable and circled through the outskirts of the town till he reached the trail leading to Jericho Valley. He rode at a good pace, estimating he should reach the gorge mouth around midnight when everybody most likely would be asleep. Twice he left the trail and took shelter in a thicket as groups of miners rode past headed for the diversion Sotol had to offer.

The moon was brightening the eastern slant of the sky when he reached the valley mouth, but its beams would not penetrate the gorge for an hour or more, working in well with his plans. Slade didn't follow the trail up the valley, but chose a route parallel to it and a mile or so to the west. Here there was scant chance of meeting anybody and what noise Shadow's irons made would not reach the miners' encampment close to the east wall.

With the plainsman's uncanny sense of distance and direction, plus landmarks he had noted on his first trip up the gorge, he pulled to a halt very nearly opposite the cabin occupied by Russ Berry and his two companions. He turned west and rode as far as he thought advisable, concealed Shadow in a convenient thicket and stole forward on foot. Several times he heard a warning buzz nearby and each time stood motionless until the alarmed snake had time to slither away. He did not greatly fear that a rattler would be able to strike above his boot tops but preferred not to take unnecessary chances.

Rounding a clump of brush that grew on the west bank of the little stream, he saw, through a fringe of growth, that a light burned in the cabin that was just across the creek.

The water was shallow, hardly coming to his knees at the deepest point, and he forded the stream without mishap. For several minutes he stood in the shadow of a final stand of bush and studied the cabin. Gradually his keen hearing registered a sound — the sound of voices muffled by the walls and the closed door. He waited another moment, then glided on, coming to a halt against the wall of the shack and close to the lighted window. With the greatest caution he edged along the wall until he was in a position to peer in. As his eyes focused to the light he saw Russ Berry and his two companions, Bayles and Courtney, seated at a table playing cards. Bottles and glasses rested on the table and to all appearances they were making a night of it, which was hardly to be expected of men who had been digging in a stuffy mine tunnel all day. And they did not look at all fatigued.

Satisfied that the trio was absorbed in their drinks and the cards, he circled the cabin and stole on till he reached the tunnel. It was not far from the shack but hidden from it by a shoulder of rock.

He approached the black mouth with considerable trepidation, although he did not believe that he had another deadfall to fear. Berry would hardly have rigged a second one after the disastrous results attendant to the first, but there was no telling what other sort of a devilish trap he might have contrived. And although he had not heard of Berry having other than two companions working with him, there might possibly be still another man guarding the burrow.

These thoughts impinged on his active imagination unpleasantly as he edged toward the silent opening that was a blacker shadow amid the shadows and as he drew nearer took on the semblance of the yawning mouth of some huge prehistoric beast waiting to engulf its prey.

Just outside the tunnel he halted to stand peering and listening. He saw nothing, heard nothing. Encouraged by the lack of sound or movement he crept cautiously under the overhanging arch of the burrow and halted again. Turning, he studied the ground he had covered, dimly visible in the wan light of the stars and the reflected glow of the moon that had not yet topped the eastern cliffs. The brush-studded terrain lay deserted. In the great stillness the prattle of the little stream rose with musical clarity. Slade again turned to the tunnel and took another cautious step. Pausing, he fumbled a candle from his pocket and struck a match, carefully shielding the flame with his hands. He touched it to the candlewick which sputtered, caught, burned with a steady glow by which he surveyed the floor, walls and roof of the tunnel.

Tonight there was no rope stretched across the bore, no signs of any kind of a trap, so far as he could see. The walls and roof were roughly shored. One thing struck him at once. To all appearances the tunnel had been begun quite a while before, several months at the least.

For some minutes he stood studying the prospect ahead, carefully examining floor, walls and roof for some cleverly-concealed snare or method of warning the inhabitants of the cabin that somebody was fooling around the bore. Finally he concluded that there was nothing of the sort to fear. And after all, it was a bit unlikely that Berry would resort to some such stratagem again. Another "accident" in his holding would be regarded somewhat askance. In fact, the coroner's jury had specifically warned him against any more shenanigans of that sort. Summing up his courage he advanced slowly, his eyes searching for anything out of the ordinary.

But aside from the fact that all indications pointed to no recent excavations in the tunnel, there appeared to be nothing of interest apparent. He carefully estimated the distance he covered and reckoned he was some twenty yards from the mouth of the bore when he came upon the first evidence of work having been done at a much later date than that of the tunnel's inception. There was loose gravel on the floor and the sides and roof had a raw look and the shoring timbers were new. But to his astonishment, this condition prevailed for little more than a couple of yards. He halted staring at a blank end wall that had been but surface scarred by pick and shovel.

What the devil did it mean? It would have taken three men only a few days to remove the earth and gravel that had recently been excavated. And Berry was supposed to have been working the claim for nearly two months, according to what Sam Yelverton had said.

With the greatest care he went over every foot of the ground. There were no indications of anything out of the ordinary. A few scoops full of gravel had been removed, and that was all. He sampled the earth and gravel of the end wall and arrived at another surprising conclusion. Of course it was impossible to tell to a certainty by such a superficial examination, but he was very much of the opinion that the gravel bank contained no gold and never had. In fact, it wasn't really a gravel bank, as were the lower slopes from which men were taking metal. Here the upper shale extended downward to what must at one time have been the river bed. The gravel admixture was slight, and it was the lower gravel banks deposited by the rushing water that produced gold. Slade was pretty much convinced that the original tunnel, dug when Berry first staked the claim, or possibly even before he took possession, was a dry hole and never produced anything of value. Yet it was an indubitable fact that Berry had been bringing in gold in large quantities.

Berry's reason for not wanting anybody nosing around his tunnel and giving it a careful once-over was now fairly apparent. Or at least under present conditions the reason was obvious. Of course formerly there may have been another and more weighty reason. But one angle was pretty well-established: the tunnel was in the nature of a blind to cover up whatever operations, doubtless off-color, that Berry was mixed up in.

At length, confident there was nothing more of interest to be discovered, he retraced his steps. Deep in thought, he was not far from the tunnel mouth when he abruptly realized he was still carrying the lighted candle. He hurriedly extinguished it and thrust the stub in his pocket.

Small though the candle flame was, in the pitch black tunnel it cast a brilliant light. Slade was momentarily blinded by the sudden transition as he groped his way slowly to the tunnel mouth. Just as he reached it, a man loomed huge against the stars. Slade caught a gleam of metal and lunged frantically for the gun. He caught the man's wrist, slewed sideways as the gun blazed. The bullet grazed his cheek. Again he was blinded by the gush of flame. With all his strength he swung the fellow around. Breast to breast they struggled in the black dark. The gun went off again, the tunnel walls rocking to the reverberations set up by the explosion. Overhead the shattered roof groaned and creaked. Another blast of vibrations and it would very likely come down and bury both battlers under tons of rock.

Slade could have drawn his own gun and shot the other, but he refrained from doing so. For all he knew the man might be an innocent miner who had seen the flicker of candlelight in the tunnel and had come to investigate. He twisted his wrist with all his strength, but the muscles swelled under his fingers and the gun barrel came slowly around toward his face. So far not a word had been spoken. In grim silence the struggling pair fought, and Slade knew that for him the forfeit of loss would be death. In a despairing effort he again swung his antagonist around and lashed out with his left hand toward where he figured the other's jaw should be, all his two hundred pounds of muscular weight behind the blow.

His fist connected with a force that jarred his arm to the shoulder. The man groaned and went limp, the gun clattering to the rock floor. As Slade let go his wrist he fell sideways and lay still.

Slade bounded out of the tunnel, conscious that shouts were sounding nearby. As he foamed across the stream a gun blazed and he felt the wind of the passing bullet.

A whole fusillade of shots followed, with bullets zipping by like angry hornets with places to go. Slade still untouched, scrambled up the bank and headed for where he had left Shadow at a dead run. If there were any snakes in his path they would have to look out for themselves. He didn't have any time to waste on them. Bullets slashed the branches overhead or spatted on the ground. Somebody was following his progress by the crashing of the brush. Gasping for breath he tore into the thicket, swung himself into the saddle and sent Shadow storming west. Behind him the aroused valley buzzed and bumbled like a disturbed hive of giant bees. Slade covered a mile with Shadow going at a gallop, then swerved south, riding as fast as he dared over the broken ground. He had no way of knowing how far down the valley the alarm would extend and if the enraged miners cut across ahead of him there would be no chance to identify himself or explain. They would shoot first and talk afterward, and the moon was now up and providing good shooting light.

Over to the right a gun banged and a slug whined past. It was followed by another and another. Slade leaned low in the saddle and urged Shadow to greater speed, heedless of rocks, bushes and other obstructions. With a sigh of relief he realized that the shooting was now behind him. Looked like he had gotten ahead of the alarm. Just the same he took no chances and didn't really breathe freely till they charged from the valley mouth and curved around to reach to Mojo Trail that led to Sotol.

Chapter Thirteen

Despite its hectic aftermath, Slade was quite pleased with the results of his exploration of the tunnel. He had established, to his own satisfaction, at least, that Russ Berry certainly wasn't digging his gold from the claim as he purported to be doing. Where did he get it? That was another question.

Slade didn't have the answer to that one, but he did have a theory, in the nature of a hunch, as it were, but foundationed on the fairly proven fact that the gold Berry kept bringing to town did *not* come from the claim and the undisputed fact that whoever was robbing the miners and the shippers had to dispose of their ill-gotten gains in some manner that would not excite suspicion. What more logical way than to pass off the stolen dust and nuggets as honestly dug in Jericho Valley? If Berry and his partners were the robbers, and Slade was very much of the opinion that they were, they had a very nearly fool-proof scheme so long as nobody was able to prove they did not dig the gold from their claim. Slade felt that he was in a position to prove they did not, but he was still not in a position to link them with the crimes that had been committed.

And gradually another conviction had been building up in his mind. Berry and his companions, Bayles and Courtney, were not alone in the business. Somewhere was a smarter man who pulled the strings from behind the scenes. Berry, Courtney and Bayles, and perhaps one or two others, might be the field men who actually committed the robberies, but Slade did not believe Berry was in a position to get the advance information the robbers certainly, on more than one occasion, had been able to tie onto. Who was the mysterious individual who provided the information and no doubt planned the robberies? Slade had not the slightest notion. Well, it was up to him to find out; that's what he was here for.

It was getting along toward the morning hours when Slade reached Sotol, but business in the saloons and gambling houses was roaring along as usual. After stabling Shadow, he entered the Dun Cow which was crowded. An affable bartender served him and passed a few jovial words.

"Don't see Arnold," Slade remarked, glancing toward the gold-weighing counter, from which the scales had been removed.

"Oh, he's out somewhere getting a breath of air," the barkeep replied. "He does a lot of riding around. Goes over to visit Wes Hargrove or some other of the ranchers every now and then. Got a notion he's of a mind to buy a spread if he can find one for sale. Used to be a cowhand, and I reckon you know a cowhand ain't ever real happy if he can't look across a steer's back every so often. Wouldn't be surprised if Crane ends up a cattleman. He's making money here, but I don't think he's over happy in this kind of a place. I rec'lect him saying once that the only reason he ever got to dealing cards in saloons was because right at the time there wasn't anything else he could tie onto."

Slade nodded. It looked that his surmise relative to Arnold was correct. Arnold did plan to sell out sometime in the near future. He was evidently doing the ground work to make the deal look logical. Then when the Jericho Valley claims petered out, nobody could accuse him of unloading the business onto a buyer at far above what it would then be worth. Yes, Arnold had plenty of wrinkles on his horns. Well, it appeared such things were condoned by the gambling profession to which Arnold belonged. Slade said good-night to the bartender and headed for bed.

The following morning when he came downstairs, Slade found old Frank Nance, the stable and roominghouse owner, sitting smoking in the little office. He accepted an invitation to set and gab a bit before going to breakfast.

"Son," old Frank asked after a few casual remarks, "have you had any more trouble like what happened the first night you were here? I was just wondering if these hellions were keeping after you."

Slade rolled and lighted a cigarette before replying. He was deciding something in his mind. Finally he nodded. "Yes," he said. "They made another try for me just the other day — up north of Jericho Valley."

He briefly outlined his experience. Nance listened in silence, then wagged his grizzled head.

"A bad bunch," he declared. "Almighty bad. Son, if I were you I'd trail my twine out of this infernal section."

"Later, perhaps, but I don't propose to be run out," Slade replied quietly.

Nance didn't appear surprised. "Hardly

figured you for the running kind," he admitted, "but just the same I 'low you're taking a chance in sticking around."

Slade proceeded to put into practice the decision at which he had arrived. "Frank," he said, "would you mind answering a few questions?"

"Not at all," the old man replied. "Go to it."

"What do you know about Russ Berry?"

"Not over much," Nance admitted. "I never paid much attention to him. He showed up here better'n two months back. I remember that because it was just a little while after Crane Arnold bought the Dun Cow from Sam Yelverton and not long before Ben Sutler disappeared. I remember mostly because right after Arnold started running the Dun Cow he had a row with Berry over his misbehaving and told him he'd have to mend his ways or stay out of the place. Berry started to get his bristles up but Cliff Yates who was working for Arnold then was right beside Crane and ready to back him up. Reckon Berry figured it wouldn't be good judgment to tackle both of them. Anyhow he cooled down and 'cept for one row in which he wasn't altogether to blame, he's always behaved himself pretty well in the Dun Cow after that."

Nance stuffed his pipe with tobacco, got it going good and resumed. "Not long after he showed here, Berry went up into Jericho Valley and staked out an old tunnel some other fellers had started and gave up for no good. Berry said the ground looked good to him, and I reckon he was right. Anyhow it wasn't long before he'd struck it rich and has been bringing out gold ever since. He brought in three fellers to work with him and they been coining money hand over fist."

"Three?" Slade interrupted. "I thought there were only two?"

"Only two now but there used to be three," Nance repeated. "The other feller left about the time you showed up here, that very same day if I rec'lect right. Berry said he was heading back to California where he had people. He was a scrawny little jigger with a hooked nose and the keenest-looking pair of eyes I ever saw in a man's head. I remember him because of those eyes. They were real light blue colored, the kind of eyes the old-timers called killer eyes. They 'lowed that all the old-time gunfighters had that kind of eyes. I wouldn't know about that, but I know I wouldn't want to see that feller's eyes looking at me across gun sights."

"I doubt if you would have enjoyed it,"

Slade observed grimly. He was thinking of slugs whining down from the rim of the Mojo Trail canyon, fired with deadly aim at a distance of nearly a thousand yards.

Nance nodded, evidently not noting Slade's use of the past tense of the verb.

"Berry's a suspicious cuss," he resumed, "always figuring somebody is out to rob him. That's why he rigged up that fool deadfall that killed poor Clem Baxter. Guess that's about all I know about Berry."

Slade nodded without comment. Nance smoked for a couple of minutes in silence, eyeing Slade contemplatively.

"Son, you 'pear to take considerable interest in the goings-on hereabouts," he observed suddenly. "I'm going to tell you something else you may find interesting, something I've never told but one other feller, and he's dead. It's about Ben Sutler's gold."

"Yes?" Slade prompted expectantly.

"Uh-huh, Ben Sutler's gold," Nance repeated. "Son, old Ben never dug that gold in Jericho Valley. Maybe it came from Jericho Valley originally, I don't know, but Ben never dug it there, and he never dug it any place else."

"Now what do you mean by that?" Slade asked.

"Ben may have dug the first poke or two he brought in, but not what he brought in later," Nance said. "Son, I did considerable prospecting when I was young, before I decided there was an easier way to make a living. I know about all there is to know about placer and drift mining. Those fellers up in Jericho Valley don't. There ain't no experienced miners up there, leastwise no drift or placer miners. Now I'll tell you something. No gold is bright and shiny before it's polished up by a jeweler, but gold that's dug out of the ground is soft and yellow and rich-looking. Gold that's laid out in the open for a long spell, years and years, is dull like — looks more like copper than gold, in fact. You might think it was copper 'cept for the difference in weight. Well, that's the kind of gold Ben Sutler brought in. I noticed it the first time I saw it, and I saw plenty more he brought in, and it was always the same. I didn't say anything because I figured where he got it and how was Ben's affair."

For a moment Slade sat silent, digesting what he had just heard. Abruptly he asked a question, "You say you told one other fellow what you've just told me?"

"That's right," said Nance. "Just one other feller and he's dead. Sheriff Clem Baxter and me got to talking about Ben Sutler and his not showing up, and I suggested to Clem that maybe it was because Ben didn't have any more gold to bring in and was ashamed to come back busted again after all the swallerforkin' he'd been doing. Clem asked me why I thought that and I told him about the kind of gold Ben used to bring in. He all of a sudden seemed mighty interested. Asked me if I was plumb sure about it. I told him I was. He didn't say anything more — Clem never was the talking kind — and then just a couple of days later he went off and got killed under that deadfall."

Slade nodded and rolled another cigarette. "Ever see any more gold of that sort brought in?" he asked casually.

"Can't say I have," Nance replied, "but then I ain't paid much attention to what's brought in. As I told you, I got over my prospecting darn foolishness years ago. I turned down a chance to stake a claim in Jericho Valley. I'm making a living and that's enough for an old feller like me. I wouldn't go poking around in that darn snakehole just to maybe tie onto a lot of money I don't need and wouldn't know what to do with if I had it. Chances are, though, nobody else has brought in any of that sort of gold, unless they happened on a spot where some nuggets had been washed out of the ground by water and had laid on the surface for a long time. That happens sometimes, you know, but usually there isn't much showing above ground."

"I expect you're right about that," Slade agreed, knowing very well that Nance was right. "Thanks for telling me what you did, Frank, it was very interesting."

He let the full force of his level gray eyes rest on the oldster's face. "And now, Frank, I want to tell you something," he said softly. "Don't under any circumstances repeat to anybody what you just told me. Keep it under your hat unless and until I tell you it's safe to do otherwise. If what you told me gets to the wrong pair of ears, your life ain't worth a busted cartridge. So don't talk to anybody, because you can't be sure it isn't the wrong somebody."

Old Frank stared at him, his jaw dropping. "Son," he said, a bit of a quaver in his voice, "the way you said that sort of gives me the creeps, but I'm taking your advice even though I don't know what the devil you mean. From now on I never heard of Ben Sutler and never saw him bring in any gold. Don't know for sure if he ever did or not."

Slade chuckled, although he was in no

mood for mirth. "Keep on feeling that way and stay alive," he said. "Well, I'm heading for the Dun Cow and some breakfast. Join me?"

"Ain't got no appetite right now," grunted Nance. "Was hungry a minute ago but I ain't any more."

"You will be again," Slade predicted smilingly. "If you don't put it off too long you'll find me over there with a surroundin' in front of me. I am hungry."

Slade walked slowly after he left the roominghouse, pondering what he had learned. There was not the slightest doubt in his mind now but that Russ Berry had in some way managed to find Ben Sutler's secret hoard. That's where the weathered gold he brought in came from. What did he do with Sutler when he "jumped" the old man's claim? There was no doubt in Slade's mind about that, either. He had murdered Sutler, of course. He would never have left the prospector alive. Ben Sutler was a dead man, despite Sam Yelverton's feeling that he was still alive.

Walt Slade was not given to theatrical gestures of any kind, but his fists clenched as he thought of the crimes for which he believed Russ Berry to be responsible. Berry was a devil in human form if there ever was one, and as yet he had not the slightest idea how he was to bring the hellion to justice.

Slade called it breakfast, but it came nearer being a noontime lunch; he had slept late. The saloon was pretty well crowded and there was plenty of animated conversation going on. He suppressed a grin as he listened to what a miner evidently just in from the valley was telling a bartender.

"The blasted thieves were snoopin' around Russ Berry's claim," he said. "Must have been a dozen of 'em from the noise they made getting away. Chuck Bayles spotted 'em and tangled with one. Threw a couple of shots at him. But the sidewinder slammed Bayles alongside the jaw with a hunk of rock or a crowbar or something like that and darn near killed him. His jaw is all swole up as big as your head. We heard 'em tearin' down the valley and threw some lead at them, but they got away. I tell you there ain't never going to be no law in this section till we organize a vigilante committee and hang somebody."

"Who do you figure to hang?" asked the bartender.

"I don't know," the miner replied. "Reckon most anybody'll do as a sort of lesson to the rest of the sidewinders."

Slade was abruptly in no grinning mood. The miner's talk was ominous, representing a mounting resentment that very little provocation could cause to flare into explosive violence. With very likely a tragic miscarriage of justice as the result. Something had to be done to remedy the situation, and without delay and he had not the slightest notion what to do or how to do it.

All very well to be convinced in his own mind that Russ Berry was guilty of robbery and murder, but proving it was something else again. He couldn't identify Berry as taking part in the killings, and you can't identify raw gold, either. So far Berry, guilty though he might be, was very much in the clear.

Uncovering his deception relative to his claim wouldn't help much. Very likely Berry, or whoever was doing his thinking for him, would come up with some plausible explanation as to where he got the gold he kept bringing in. And even though he couldn't explain it to everybody's satisfaction there would still be nothing concrete to pin on him. Recalling his "confession" in the death of the Sheriff Baxter, it was not beyond imagination that Berry might "confess" again, admitting that he hoped to unload a worthless claim on somebody, just as it had been unloaded on him, and had been implying that he got the gold from the dry hole with that object in mind. And you can't lock a man up for meditating deception. Yes, he might as well admit it, he had no case on Berry and, he morosely conceded, the prospects for getting one on him at the moment appeared dim. He finished his breakfast and went for a walk in the open air, where he could always think better.

Chapter Fourteen

Sotol was full of surprises. It had one ready for Walt Slade. He was strolling along the main street when he observed Deputy Tom Horrel hurrying across to intercept him.

"Was looking for you," Horrel said. "They'd like to have a word with you over at the sheriff's office."

"Okay," Slade agreed and followed the deputy. When they arrived at the office he found Sheriff Yates, Crane Arnold, Sam Yelverton, Wes Hargrove and Doc Cooper seated around the desk looking very solemn.

"Found him, eh, Tom?" Hargrove remarked. "Have a seat, son," he nodded to Slade.

Slade sat down and waited expectantly. Hargrove did the talking.

"Son," he said, "I reckon you've noticed that things have been going sort of bad since you landed in this section. They'd been going bad for quite a spell but they seemed to have picked up of late. Fact is there are too darn many owlhoots squatting in this section, brought in by the gold strike of course. Well, we've decided on something that needs to be done. Sheriff Yates and Arnold thought of it first and the rest of us agreed to string along with them; we figure it's the thing to do. Doc and Sam and me are the commissioners, you know with the authority to act." He paused, cleared his throat and speculated Slade a moment.

There was an amused light in Slade's gray eyes. Here it comes, he thought. El Halcon! get out of town! He was totally unprepared for what did come.

"Yes, we decided something had to be done," resumed Hargrove. "It 'pears you're the only gent hereabouts who has been able to down one of the sidewinders and wing a couple more. And the way you slid out of that trap they laid for you at the roominghouse was mighty slick, too. We figure if anybody can give the devils their comeuppance, you can. There's a vacancy in the sheriff's office and we think you're just the man to fill it. So we're offering you a job as deputy sheriff to give Cliff the hand he needs, and we hope you'll take it."

Slade dissembled his surprise. "But aren't you taking a chance in offering an important post like that to a stranger?" he demurred.

Old Sam Yelverton chuckled. "Reckon you aren't so much of a stranger hereabouts any more," he said with a meaning aimed at Slade's ears alone.

"We don't look on you as a stranger," Hargrove added. "We've all taken considerable of a shine to you and figure we're not making a mistake. So what do you say?"

Slade made up his mind swiftly. The proposition was not without its attractions. It would give him a needed excuse for hanging around the section and would enable him to act officially if necessary without revealing his Ranger connections, which he preferred not to do at present. Also he didn't see how it could restrict his movements to any great degree.

"Okay," he said, "I'll take the job, with a condition."

"What's the condition?" Hargrove asked.

"That if I set out to handle a chore I'll be allowed to handle it as I see fit, without interference from anybody."

Hargrove glanced at Sheriff Yates, who hesitated an instant, then nodded.

"Can't see anything wrong with the condition," said Hargrove. "All right, we'll let it go at that. Hold up your right hand."

Another moment and Slade was sworn in

as a deputy sheriff of the county. Sheriff Yates drew something from a drawer.

"Here's your badge," he said, passing it to Slade. "Wear it or keep it in your pocket, as you like. Tom hardly ever wears his unless he's on business."

"Think I'll keep it in my pocket for the present," Slade decided, stowing it away.

"And now I vote we all go over to the Dun Cow and have a drink on it," said Yelverton.

Nobody objected to that and they left the office in a group.

Slade was still considerably surprised at the unexpected turn of events, but after a few minutes reflection he was less so. Hargrove said that Sheriff Yates and Crane Arnold first advanced the proposition, but Slade wondered if old Sam Yelverton, knowing him to be a Ranger and thinking to lend him a helping hand, hadn't cleverly planted the thought in Yates' mind. Yes, doubtless that was the answer. Well, he didn't see how it could do him any harm and might work to his advantage.

During the few days that followed, Slade found his duties as deputy sheriff very light. Jericho Valley was peaceful, no robberies occurring and no violence. There were a few friendly fights and cuttings in Sotol but they were to be expected and did not give the authorities much cause for concern. It was admitted that the boys had to let off steam now and then and so long as nobody was killed, little attention was given to such rukuses. Two gold shipments, both handled by Crane Arnold, went through to the railroad without mishap.

"Looks like the hellions have learned who the new deputy is and aren't taking any chances," Sam Yelverton said jokingly to Slade. "But," he added, "I seem to rec'lect an old saying about the calm before the storm. Maybe that's what it is."

"Very likely you have the right of it there," Slade conceded. "Well, if you're in the mood for quotations, let's hope for the best and be prepared for the worst."

It was the evening following this conversation that Slade made his astonishing discovery. He was standing at the Dun Cow bar, watching the crowd and listening to stray scraps of conversation, when Sheriff Clifton Yates came in, nodded to Slade and hurried to where Crane Arnold lounged against the gold-weighing counter. He leaned across the counter and began talking earnestly to Arnold who leaned forward to catch what he was saying. Slade idly regarded the pair.

Suddenly he tensed, his eyes narrowing.

He stared at Yates and Arnold. "Well, I'll be hanged!" he muttered. "Why the devil didn't I spot it before?"

Intently he studied the two men and arrived at a startling conclusion. Ever since he first laid eyes on Crane Arnold, Slade had been haunted by a conviction that he had recently met somebody who greatly resembled the saloonkeeper. Abruptly he knew who that somebody was.

Crane Arnold and Clifton Yates, especially when seen in profile, had all the appearance of being identical twins. The color of the hair was different, and Slade shrewdly suspected the hair of one or the other was dyed, but otherwise, aside from the fact that Yates wore a mustache and Arnold did not, the resemblance was astounding. In feature, gesture and expression they were the same. If they weren't brothers, they should be. Slade firmly believed they were. He studied them a little longer, noting that the smooth swift movements of the hands of the one were the counterpart of the other's and that each had the like mannerism of hunching one shoulder slightly when making a remark. Yes, there was no doubt about it, the two men were closely related. Cousins, possibly, but Slade was confident that they were much more apt to be brothers. He turned and walked out of the saloon. He wanted to be alone to think without interruption. His mind was in considerable of a whirl and he desired to settle down and properly evaluate what he had just learned. Certain things that had been very hazy were rapidly becoming startlingly clear.

Reaching his room, Slade drew a chair to the window and rolled a cigarette. He sat looking out at the stars and not seeing them.

In the course of his Ranger experience, Slade had learned that men who pretended to be something other than what they were usually had something to conceal. And that men who concealed something very often "had" other things that would not bear scrutiny. Just what reason did Yates and Arnold have for keeping under cover a relationship that undoubtedly existed? Why did they pose as strangers when they first met in Sotol? He recalled Sam Yelverton mentioning that Yates had showed up in Sotol shortly after Arnold took over the Dun Cow and that Arnold had hired him as a dealer, soon raising him to a sort of assistant, in the nature of a manager, to help him run the place before he eased him into the sheriff's office. Just what was their game, anyhow?

Painstakingly, he went over all he had learned relative to the two men and their activities, and things that appeared unimportant at the time abruptly acquired significance.

He recalled Yates' agitation when he described the robbery of the gold wagon in the canyon, and his anxiety as to whether he, Slade, had gotten a close look at the robbers. He also recalled that Yates had appeared relieved when he mentioned that the man he shot from the canyon rim was smashed out of human semblance by the thousand-foot fall. Abruptly Russ Berry's lack of concern when he met Slade face to face in the Dun Cow after having every reason to believe that he had been drowned in the river west of Jericho Valley was explained. That afternoon, after contacting Slade, Yates had hurriedly ridden to the valley, ostensibly to investigate the murder of the miner whose body had been brought in earlier in the day. Very likely Yates had informed Berry that his supposed victim was still very much alive.

Crane Arnold's acceptance, without comment, of the weathered gold Russ Berry kept bringing in also assumed importance. Arnold knew very well, of course, that Berry never dug that gold from his shale-bank claim. And Slade was very much of the opinion that Arnold also knew perfectly well where that gold came from.

Also to be considered was the fact that Arnold's gold shipments always went through without mishap and arrived safely at the railroad town, while other shippers experienced loss despite their efforts to keep secret the time and manner in which they transported their metal. Arnold as a respected businessman of the community and Yates in the sheriff's office were in a position to obtain information denied folks in general. Small things in themselves, but looming large in the aggregate.

Yes, there was little doubt but that Crane Arnold was the brains behind Russ Berry and his companion thieves. Slade exasperatedly admitted to himself that he had carelessly overlooked obvious details that pieced together into a very simple pattern. Clear enough now was the explanation of the unlooked for ingenuity displayed by Berry in his "confession" of his responsibility for Sheriff Baxter's death. The clever Arnold had at once realized what the stupid Berry did not, that somebody might note evidence that Baxter never fell from the cliff top and start a train of investigation that could eventually lead to Berry and expose his worthless claim. Arnold had told Berry what to do and Berry had followed orders with successful results, his story being accepted without question.

Explained, too, was the attempt on his life here in the roominghouse. Yates, perhaps believing that Slade had not told him all he knew of the gold-wagon robbery, had directed him to the place, planning to eliminate him before he had a chance to do much talking. A snake-blooded bunch of scoundrels, all right, and with plenty of savvy. And his unexpected elevation to the post of deputy sheriff now took on a very sinister look. Beyond question, Arnold and Yates had some scheme in mind and it behooved him to be very much on his guard.

Of course it was barely possible that the two men had a legitimate reason for concealing their relationship and were it not for the other angles involved, Slade would have been inclined to give them the benefit of the doubt. But as the situation stood, the revelation had provided the impetus that started his thought processes functioning to carefully evaluate all incidents in which Yates and Arnold had been directly or indirectly involved. His ultimate conclusion was that Crane Arnold was the brains behind the owlhoot bunch operating in the section. Now the big question was, To what use could he put what he had learned? Slade didn't know. He would have to trail along, hoping that developments would provide him with opportunity.

Chapter Fifteen

Slade was just finishing breakfast the following morning when Deputy Tom Horrel came hurrying in.

"Cliff wants you over at the office," he announced. "He's got a tip that some suspicious characters are hanging out in an old abandoned miner's cabin down to the southwest. That's hole-in-the-wall country down there and a favorite hide-out for owlhoots. Sheriff Baxter nabbed several there. Him and Cliff came nigh to dropping a loop on some wide-loopers who were holed up in that very cabin a while back, but they gave him the slip by circling around by way of a trail fork. Cliff figures to take that into consideration this time and plug the bolt hole. This may be the big chance we've been hoping for."

Slade accompanied Horrel to the office where Yates and two more deputies were waiting.

"Get your horse," Yates directed. "We'll ride pronto."

Slade threw the rig on Shadow and they set out, heading south by a little west. Soon they were riding across good rangeland dotted with numerous clumps of cattle, many of which bore Wes Hargrove's Bradded H brand.

Clifton Yates gestured to a range of rugged hills cutting across the distant southern skyline.

"That's where the hellions swoop down from to grab off stock," he explained for Slade's benefit. "Trails down there leading to the lower Big Bend country and if they get a headstart it's darn near impossible to catch up with them. They know every crack and hole in that upended section. The cowhand who brought me word said there were seven holed up in that cabin, tough-looking customers that so far as he could see didn't have any business there. I figure they plan a raid, tonight maybe. If we can get the jump on them I think we shouldn't have too much trouble rounding them up. A bunch fooled Baxter and me down there one time, but I aim to put it over on this bunch."

Slade nodded in silence. They rode on and after a couple of hours were climbing a long slope, the trail winding up to pour into a saw-edged notch in the crest of the sag. Here the going was hard, the horses proceeding at little better than a walk. Finally they reached the notch and rode through it to where the south slope began. To the left the sag stretched up to a rounded skyline and was heavily brush-grown. And only a few hundred yards from the notch the trail forked, the east fork following the slope, the west branch turning to sidle down it and vanish around a jut of cliff. Yates pulled up and issued his orders.

"You'll stay here, Slade," he directed. "Keep your eyes skun and watch that east fork. The rest of us will follow the west fork that leads to the cabin. It curves around the cabin and crosses the east fork about three miles below here. If the trail is watched and they spot us coming, I figure they'll head back along the east fork and on into the east hills where they'll be safe. Holed up here you should be able to hold them off — they can't round the bulge there against gunfire. If there's nobody in the cabin when we get there, we'll hightail back as fast as we can. We'd ought to get here by the time the ball opens, if it does. Got everything straight?"

"Everything okay," Slade replied. As the posse headed down the west fork he hooked his leg comfortably over the horn, fished out the makin's and began rolling a cigarette.

But the instant the others had vanished around a bulge of cliff, he let paper and tobacco fall to the ground, dismounted and led Shadow into the brush that flanked the trail on the east. He quickly hunted out a dense thicket and forced the big black into the heart of it, dropping the split reins to the ground as a warning not to move. He knew the animal would not stray and hoped he wouldn't take a sudden notion to sing a song. However, he did not worry much on that score, Shadow usually being a very silent horse.

"I'm playing a hunch," he told the black. "This whole business has a fishy smell. Sounds straight enough and the logical way for Yates to handle the affair. Ordinarily I wouldn't think anything of it, but things being what they are, I figure it's best for us not to take any chances. If my hunch is a straight one, we'll have a showdown mighty soon. Take it easy, now, and for Pete's sake, keep quiet!"

Confident that Shadow would do so, he eased back to where he could watch both the trail and the brush-grown slope and lay down in the shade of a thick bush, where he would be practically invisible to anyone on the trail or the slope.

Fifteen dragging minutes passed, increased to twenty, edged toward the half hour. Slade lay motionless, his eyes fixed on the slope, his ears attuned to any sound that might come from the trail.

Suddenly from a bush no great distance up the sag a startled bird shot up like a popgun ball. Slade lay perfectly motionless, watching and waiting. He was not at all surprised when two men materialized from the growth, stealing along silently as Indians.

Nor was he particularly surprised when he recognized Russ Berry's two partners, Chuck Bayles and Pete Courtney.

Pausing often to peer and listen, Courtney and Bayles glided down the slope. They reached the final fringe of brush that edged the trail and peered forth cautiously.

"Blast it, he's not in sight!" Slade heard Bayles mutter. "Now where the devil did that hellion get to? Looks like there's been a slip-up."

Slade got noiselessly to his feet and eased forward until he was within ten paces of the unheeding pair.

"Looking for somebody, boys?" he called.

Bayles and Courtney jumped a foot at the

sound of his voice, gulping in their throats. They whirled around, hands on their guns. Slade stood motionless, waiting.

It was Courtney who lost his head and tried to pull. Slade drew and shot him before he could clear leather. Bayles managed to get into action and fired wildly. Slade's answering bullet took him squarely between the eyes.

Lowering his gun, Slade walked forward and gazed down into Courtney's dead face.

"Darn!" he growled. "I meant to get the sidewinder through the shoulder and leave him in shape to do a little talking, but I pulled to the left and drilled him dead center. I must be getting a bit rusty."

He listened a moment and as no sound came from the trail he ejected the spent shells from his gun and replaced them with fresh cartridges. Working swiftly, he dragged the two bodies into a thicket and covered them with brush. Then, estimating the time he had to spare and deciding it was sufficient, he mounted Shadow and sent him up the slope in search of the horses the pair had ridden. Circling about, he found them with little difficulty, tethered to a branch. He untied and led them to the crest. Removing the rigs he tossed them under a bush and sent the horses skalley-hooting down the far slope, knowing they would fend for themselves. Then he returned to the trail, took up the position in which the posse had left him and proceeded to enjoy his belated cigarette. He was very well satisfied with the way things had worked out so far. At least he had eliminated two of the devils and at the same time banished any lingering doubt relative to Yates and Arnold.

Fully an hour elapsed before the posse reappeared, riding swiftly. Tom Horrel let out a relieved shout at the sight of Slade quietly sitting his horse, but Clifton Yates' eyes bulged and his jaw sagged. He snapped it shut and Slade saw his chest heave with the deep breath he drew.

"The hellions gave us the slip," Horrel chattered excitedly. "The stove in the shack was still warm but they weren't nowheres around. Reckon they caught on somehow and pulled out. Maybe they saw that cowhand who brought you the word riding the trail, Cliff, and decided it was best not to take chances."

"Looks that way," Yates replied in a strained voice.

"Anyhow, they sure didn't come up the trail," Slade observed. "What next?"

"Next we'll head for home," Yates growled, his brows drawing together in a scowl. "We followed a cold trail, that's all. No sense in hanging around here any longer."

Horrel and the other deputies chatted animatedly as they rode back to town, but Yates was silent, his face working from time to time, a perplexed look in his eyes. Now and then he shot a glance at Slade, who pretended not to notice. Inwardly he was bubbling with mirth over the sheriff's discomfiture. He knew Yates must be burning with curiosity as to just what had happened but didn't dare to risk an indirect question. He could almost feel sorry for the sheriff in his utter bewilderment and his futile attempts to try and figure how his well-planned try at murder had miscarried.

They reached Sotol without mishap when dusk was falling. After eating, Slade joined Sam Yelverton, Wes Hargrove and some of their cronies in a poker game. He was in a complacent mood and was formulating a plan of action he hoped to put into effect in the near future.

There was a perturbed gathering in the back room of the Dun Cow late that night. Russ Berry was there, glowering and gnawing his knuckles, and Clifton Yates, his face anxious and haggard. Crane Arnold, pacing the floor with jerky steps was not his usual urbane self. His eyes glittered and his mouth was clamped in a hard line.

"We've got to pull out," he said. "If we hang around here much longer that big hellion will maneuver us into a position where we'll have to agree to anything he says to save our necks. He's darn near got us there already. Of course he killed Courtney and Bayles! Somehow he caught on and was ready for them. No doubt in my mind as to that. We've just about cleaned up everything worth-while as it is and it's time to move on. I've got a buyer for this infernal saloon and it'll only take me a couple of days to close the deal and take care of everything else. With Bayles and Courtney out of the picture we'll have to be with you tomorrow night, Russ. One more good haul and we'll hightail and leave El Halcon holding an empty sack."

"I'd like to have just one chance first to look at that son of a mangy horned toat over gun sights," Berry growled savagely.

"You'd have about as much chance as a rabbit in a houndog's mouth," Arnold replied. "I don't believe there's a man in Texas who can shade him on the draw. I'd hesitate to take him on myself. Well, anyhow there's just the three of us to do the dividing now, which is something. You fellers get going. Use the back door. I don't want anybody seeing you leave here tonight. We'll stop at the shack tomorrow night after dark, Russ, and then join you!"

"I'm in favor of pulling out right now, tonight," quavered Yates. "Who knows what that seven-foot hellion's got up his sleeve. Tomorrow or next day may be too late."

Crane Arnold shot him a glance of contempt. "I don't see how the devil you ever came to be a brother of mine," he declared. "Your guts are water. Shut up and do what I tell you and everything will work out as it should. All right, get going. See you tomorrow night, Russ."

CHAPTER SIXTEEN

Late the following evening Slade dropped into the Dun Cow for something to eat. He dawdled over his meal, ordered a drink and sat smoking and watching the crowd. An hour or so after dark he saw Crane Arnold enter the back room and close the door behind him. Half an hour elapsed and he did not reappear. Slade waited ten minutes longer, then quietly left the saloon.

Hurrying to the stable he saddled Shadow, circled through the outskirts of the town and rode north toward desolate Jericho Valley. Upon reaching the gorge mouth, he once again left the trail and kept well to the east. The air was crisply cool and he hadn't much fear that the rattlesnakes which infested the valley would be active. They were very probably holed up somewhere out of the cold. He did not draw rein till he was opposite Russ Berry's cabin. It was lighted and from time to time he could see shadows cross the window as the occupants moved about.

An hour passed, very slowly. A gibbous moon rose above the eastern valley wall and flooded the gorge with wanly silver light. Soon objects stood out in misty detail. The cabin door opened and two men came out. The light was not strong enough to distinguish faces but there was no doubt in Slade's mind as to who they were. He wondered where Russ Berry was but lacked time and opportunity to more than wonder. He had to keep an eye on Crane Arnold and Clifton Yates.

Arnold and Yates mounted horses that stood before the cabin and rode north. Slade let them get some distance ahead before he eased Shadow forward, keeping within the gloom shrouding the brush that flanked the trail. He hoped the noise made by their own progress would drown the slight click of Shadow's irons and believed it would. He held himself ready to instantly halt the black should the horsemen ahead pull up.

Apparently they were not worried about pursuit, for they never once glanced back the way they had come. Mile after mile Slade trailed the steadily riding pair. Farther up the gorge the brush thinned and he was hard put to keep under cover. Once or twice the quarry would certainly have sighted him with a backward glance. He anxiously speculated the distorted moon. It was working across the sky toward the western rim and once it was behind the crags, keeping the pair in sight would be difficult in the extreme. To make matters worse, little clouds kept floating past and dimming the light.

The men ahead rode slowly. Apparently they were in no hurry to reach wherever they were headed for. Slade surmised that perhaps they needed daylight for whatever they had in mind. They were far up the canyon now, no great distance from the northern slope up which the trail made its way north into the farther fastnesses of the Guadalupes.

Slade began to grow acutely uneasy. If the pair planned to leave the canyon by way of the trail up the slope, following them across the spine of the hogback would be ticklish business indeed. Well nigh impossible, in fact. The moon was low in the west and soon would be beneath the horizon, but dawn was not far off and in the strengthening light he could not hope to stick close enough to the horsemen to keep them in sight and remain undetected.

Suddenly they turned their horses to the west and rode straight for the canyon wall, which was not far off. Slade pulled Shadow to a halt and watched them for a moment before also turning off. The stream now ran at no great distance from the cliffs and he would have to cross it. He must led Arnold and his companion get some distance ahead before putting Shadow to the water; a certain amount of splashing was inevitable and sound carried far in the stillness of the night. He was relieved, although he didn't know what was in the wind, when the pair abruptly halted. He watched them dismount, lead the horses to one side and behind some brush and then head for the cliffs on foot. He saw their forms dim and vanish in the gloom at the base of the wall.

Now what the devil should he do? If the two men were for some reason holed up at the cliff base, to attempt to cross the moonlit open west of the stream would be tantamount to suicide. As he gazed about perplexed, he saw something that might tend to simplify matters for him.

Two clouds were moving rapidly toward the moon, both of them very black and dense. The first cloud was small and long, the one behind big and broad. Slade absently reflected that they bore a most comical resemblance to a wagon drawn by a very long raw-boned horse. Very soon they would pass across the face of the moon.

Eager to take advantage of this unlooked for assistance, he veered Shadow into a thicket close to the stream bank and dismounted, dropping the split reins to the ground.

"Grass here, and you can get a drink if you need it," he whispered. "And darn you, keep quiet!"

He glided forward to the edge of the brush and waited. The head of the horse-cloud floated over the face of the moon. A faint twilight remained but Slade decided to take a chance. Bending nearly double, he stepped into the stream, which was shallow, quickly forded it and crept forward. As the cloud began to pass and the light strengthened, he crouched behind a boulder and waited.

The moonlight flooded down, but only for a few moments. The wagon-cloud arrived and the light went out altogether. Slade straightened up and moved ahead, careful to dislodge no stone that might make a racket. He reached the cliff face just as the light began to strengthen again and thankfully crouched in the pitch-black darkness beneath the overhang.

For long minutes he remained motionless,

listening intently. Not a sound broke the stillness, but his position was not an enviable one. For all he knew, Arnold and Yates might be squatting close by waiting for daylight. If so, to advertise his presence would be unwise to put it mildly. But as the minutes passed, it seemed beyond reason that the two men would sit there without exchanging a remark or making some sort of a move that could be heard. Again he straightened up and began edging along toward where he had seen them vanish into the gloom, leaning his shoulder against the rough cliff face, feeling his way with his outstretched hands.

Suddenly and without warning the cliff face against which he leaned his weight wasn't there any more. He lurched sideways, lost his balance. He made a despairing effort to right himself and could not, falling amid loose stones with a clatter that set the echoes to jumping. Frantically he rolled to one side, hands streaking to his guns. His face was beaded with sweat, his heart pounding. Surely anybody within several hundred yards must have heard the racket he kicked up.

But the silence resumed as unbroken as before he shattered it with his fall. Finally he rose to his feet with a disgusted exclamation. He was certain that there was nobody anywhere near. But where in the devil had Arnold and the other horned toad gotten to?

Abandoning all caution, he fumbled a match from his pocket and struck it. The tiny flare instantly explained his mishap. There was an opening in the face of the cliff, but an opening that would not be noticed by anybody passing within a few yards of the wall, for an overlapping of stone hid it from view. It was the sudden ending of the overlap that had caused him to fall.

The match flickered out. He struck another and peered into the opening, advancing a few steps. Glancing up he saw, far above, a single star shining in a narrow ribbon of moonlit sky. It was not a cave he was in, but a crevice, a narrow split in the face of the canyon wall. Ahead was thick gloom and utter silence.

The second match scorched his fingers. Slade dropped it and stood debating what to do next. Unquestionably Arnold and Yates had entered the crevice. To follow in the narrow crack was foolhardy in the extreme, for if he met them coming back the results would be unpleasantly lively, with the odds against him. But he had dealt himself cards in the game and felt that he had to play the hand out. Besides, he knew very well that his burning curiosity would not allow him to sidestep the adventure. He moved forward with the greatest caution, testing the ground ahead with each advancing foot before trusting his weight on it, brushing the rock wall with his hand.

However, the passage did not appear to be overly perilous. Apparently there were no pitfalls and only a few loose stones scattered over the rock floor. Overhead the sky was brightening with the approach of dawn and more and more light filtered into the fissure. Slade stepped out a little more briskly.

For more than an hour he followed the gigantic fissure that wound and curved till his sense of direction was utterly confused. At first he presumed it had been riven in the rock by some volcanic convulsion, but later decided it had more likely been carved by erosion weathering down a softer strata through untold ages.

Several times he passed dark openings in the rock wall, presumably caves of natural origin. At these he paused, peering and listening, but each time, decided to continue along the main crevice. Considerably more than an hour had elapsed when he noted three of the caves separated by only a brief space. Just before reaching the last of these he halted abruptly, his muscles tensing. A sound had come from it. Gradually he identified the sound as the snuffling of a horse, but the light was not yet sufficiently strong enough to penetrate more than a few feet into the burrow and he could see nothing. He took a chance, glided past the opening and continued on his uncertain way. He rounded a shallow curve and again halted. Ahead was light, much stronger than that which filtered down between the towering crevice walls.

For several moments he stood listening. He was not sure, but he thought he heard a low rumble of voices. What was ahead? he wondered. He didn't know but felt that it was very likely something dangerous. Easing forward, every nerve strained to hair-trigger alertness, he took the greatest care not to dislodge any stone or otherwise make a sound and stealthed along, step by slow step.

A tang of wood smoke stung his nostrils, mingled with another odor, an offensive scent that he could not at the moment definitely catalogue; it was like to the smell of ripe cucumbers left too long in the sun. He eased forward a little more and where the walls of the narrow corridor fell away, halted abruptly, crouching beside a jut of stone that cast a shadow upon him, rendering him invisible, he felt sure, to the occupants of the strange place that lay before his eyes.

At his feet was a narrow ledge ending in a steep slope that stretched downward some fifty feet or so to the floor of a bowl-shaped depression which was still shrouded in gloom. He glanced upward and saw an irregular circle of blue sky that pressed upon the ragged crest of the cliffs that walled the funnel-shaped depression of which the bowl floor formed the smaller end. The cliffs were broken and overhanging. Slade noted that they were basaltic with decided characteristics of lava. The funnel had been a fumarole or small volcanic crater a million or so years in the past.

Cautiously he peered around the sheltering stone. The ledge, which was so narrow at the crevice mouth, widened quickly until it achieved a breadth of ten feet or more before it narrowed again to peter out against the rock wall a dozen yards to the right.

Near the end of the ledge, at its widest part, a fire burned and around the fire squatted Crane Arnold, Clifton Yates and Russ Berry. They appeared to be staring expectantly across the bowl to where Slade could now see that a circular opening, doubtless a cave mouth, cut the stone of the opposing cliff.

Although the sky was bright with sunlight, the bottom of the great funnel still remained shrouded in darkness. Suddenly, however, a shaft of sunlight spilled over the eastern cliff and struck against the opposite wall. It fell swiftly downward, piercing the shadows and dissipating them. A moment later and the whole floor of the bowl was flooded with golden light. Slade stared at what it revealed and felt his palms suddenly moist with sweat.

Chapter Seventeen

The rock-walled bowl was a weird place in itself, but its occupants made it seem like a scene from the deepest circle of Dante's Hell.

The place was a den of rattlesnakes. There were thousands of the loathsome reptiles in view, slithering about, lying in their deadly-looped coils, twined together in repulsive balls. There was hardly a foot of the rocky floor that was not occupied by a snake.

Slade had seen similar places but never one of such size and number of occupants. No wonder Jericho Valley was alive with the lethal brutes with such a nest of them ready to hand. The bowl was perfect sanctuary and breeding place for them. The sun heated the rock walls and they stayed warm and comfortable at night and through the cold months. Probably they would be active and moving about all winter.

What in the devil was Arnold and his

companions doing in the place, he wondered, unless they were merely communing with their fellow snakes. Admirable but rather unlikely. From the looks of the fire, Berry had spent the night there. Why? Slade didn't know, but he felt that the answer was important and upon it his next move would quite likely depend.

Slade was indeed in considerable of a quandary. He had caught up with his quarry, but now that he had he didn't just know what to do about them. There was no law, so far as he knew, against men riding up a canyon and holing up in a snake pit. And no matter what he believed, he still had nothing definite on any one of the unsavory trio. Convinced though he was that Yates and Arnold had been back of the attempt on his life the day before, he couldn't prove it. Not with Courtney and Bayles dead and unable to testify to that effect. They had been associated with Berry, true, but Berry could disavow any knowledge of their activities of the day before, and he'd make it stick.

Uncertainly, Slade fumbled with his broad leather belt and from the cunningly-concealed secret pocket drew forth the famous silver star set on a silver circle, the feared and honored badge of the Texas Rangers. He pinned it to his shirt front.

Anyhow, he was ready to act as a peace officer if occasion warranted, and he had a hunch that something was going to happen soon that would give him occasion to need the authority of the illustrious corps. Crane Arnold and his companions weren't here just to watch the snakes.

As the sun warmed the rocks, the rotten-cucumber-like stench of the reptiles strengthened until it was almost unbearable. Slade had never smelt anything to equal it and hoped he never would again. Grimly he waited for something to develop. Something did.

From the dark cave mouth piercing the far cliff a figure suddenly appeared, a bent, white-haired figure bearing a large plumped out buckskin sack on bowed shoulders.

With unbelieving eyes, Slade watched the old man walk from the cave mouth and begin picking his way across the bowl. He walked very slowly, his movements unhurried, rythmic. The snakes appeared to pay him not the least mind as he stepped over them or his feet brushed past their hideous coils. It seemed utterly impossible for a man to walk through that pit of death and not get bitten a score of times, but the old fellow was doing it.

Slade suddenly recalled the stories he had

been told concerning old Ben Sutler's strange power over animals and reptiles. Here then was the explanation of Sutler's hidden gold, and of Sutler's mysterious disappearance, but Slade still couldn't believe what his eyes told him was so.

His glance shifted to the men beside the fire, who were watching the old fellow's slow progress across the deadly bowl with greedy, expectant eyes. Abruptly Slade's own eyes were the icy eyes of El Halcon as he glanced back to where Ben Sutler picked his way through that labyrinth of death, and his teeth ground together.

The old man seemed utterly worn out, stooping beneath his heavy burden. Once or twice he tottered on his feet, his step suddenly jerky, and each time a nearby snake rattled warningly.

Slade could feel sweat starting out on his face. His hands were balled into trembling fists. Every nerve was tautened to the breaking point. His muscles tensed and strained in sympathy with Sutler's faltering steps and when he weaved a little and a snake buzzed, Slade jerked spasmodically. The old man could never make it! Under the stress of utter exhaustion he was growing nervous and his nervousness was communicating to the easily excited reptiles. The secret of his power over the things was his placidity, his slow methodical movements, his utter lack of fear. Now, realizing his own condition, he was knowing fear and his power was waning. But still he weaved and shambled toward the slope, planting his feet as carefully as he could keeping his hands perfectly motionless. Once a huge rattler reared high, its jaws gaping, venom-like brown ink dripping from its raised fangs and Slade gave him up for lost. If the monster struck him he would fall to certain death.

But Sulter crept slowly past the legless horror and the snake sank down again. Slade expelled the breath he had been holding in a quivering sigh as Sutler at last reached the slope and began climbing wearily toward the ledge. When he topped the sag at last he lurched to the wall and leaned against it, gasping.

With an oath Russ Berry strode forward, jerked the filled sack from the old man's limp hands and up-ended it over a blanket spread on the ground. Over the big heap already pyramided on the blanket rained wires and nuggets of gold. Arnold and Yates crowded close, licking their lips.

Old Ben Sutler spoke from where he sagged against the wall. "Gents," he quavered, "don't send me back there again.

There's hardly any left, anyhow. I'm plumb tuckered, all nervous and wore out. I can't walk straight any more and I'm scared. The snakes know it and they're jumpy. I'll never get across again without getting bit."

Russ Berry whirled on the old man. His big hand lashed out and caught Sutler across the mouth. Old Ben fell heavily and rolled to the very edge of the pit where he lay groaning, blood from his cut lips staining his white beard. Berry glared down at him.

"What the devil!" he rumbled. "We've got about all there is and we haven't any time to waste. To the devil with what's left. We'll toss this old coot to the snakes and get going. I've a hunch the quicker we put a few mountains and rivers between us and this section the better."

The others nodded callous agreement. Berry bent over old Ben to carry out his threat. He jerked erect as if drawn by a red-hot wire as a voice rang out, "Let that man alone!"

The trio whirled to face the cleft mouth. They stared in incredulous disbelief at the grim figure towering there, the star of the Rangers gleaming on his broad breast, a gun in each hand. Walt Slade was taking no chances.

"Get your hands up!" he blared at them. "Up, I say! In the name of the State of Texas! You are under arrest for robbery and murder. Anything you say —"

He took a step to one side as he spoke, for the sunlight reflecting from the cliff face dazzled his eyes a little. His foot came down on a loose stone that rolled and he floundered for a moment off-balance.

Instantly the three acted. Clifton Yates got his gun out first, but before he could pull trigger he was gasping and writhing on the rock floor, blood pouring from his mouth and pulsing from the gaping holes in his breast. Russ Berry fired wildly and two slugs from Slade's guns seemed to hurl his huge body into the air and bring it down with a crash beside Yates.

Crane Arnold, cold, deadly, his white face a mask of hate and fury, took deliberate aim. Slade reeled and almost fell as the bullet ripped his side. A second slug burned a red streak along his bronzed cheek. He fired again and again, but Arnold was weaving and ducking, an elusive mark against the blinding glare of the sunlight pouring into the funnel. Back and back he glided, with El Halcon grim, relentless, following with blazing guns.

A slug slashed through the flesh of Slade's

upper arm and again he reeled off-balance. Arnold's eyes blazed with triumph as he steadied his gun. He took one more step backward and his heels hit against the prostrate form of old Ben Sutler. He tried to whirl around and save himself, but a gnarled hand grabbed his ankle and jerked. He lost his balance completely, pitched sideways and over the lip of the ledge onto the steep slope. With a yell of terror he rolled and bounded toward the floor of the bowl and crashed in among the snakes. A perfect inferno of rattles and hisses quivered the air.

Arnold struggled to his knees and a snake struck him in the face. Another and another struck him. He screamed with pain as the needle-sharp fangs pierced his flesh. With a mighty effort he gained his feet. The awful fear that contorted his writhing features suddenly changed to insane rage. Yelling and mouthing, he jerked a second gun from a shoulder holster and fired madly at the rearing coffin heads all around him, the reports blending in a veritable drumroll of sound which the great funnel, a natural megaphone, magnified a thousand-fold. The rock walls shuddered to the pound of the tossing vibrations.

Crane Arnold screamed again, a hitch-pitched shriek of rage and agony. The awful sound was suddenly drowned in a thundering roar. Walt Slade instinctively glanced upward and saw the huge overhang of the far cliff split away and rush downward in an avalanche of splintered stone. He bounded forward, jerked old Ben Sutler to his feet and rushed him toward the cleft mouth just as the falling mass hit the floor of the bowl with a crash that shook the mountains.

Slade dived into the shelter of the cleft, dragging the helpless Sutler with him. Fragments of stone stung their flesh, huge lumps slammed against the cliff wall with the force of bullets and shattered there; but they hugged the side of the cleft and escaped serious injury. Outside, the bowl rocked and reeled as other overhangs became detached and thundered down.

Abruptly the turmoil ceased. A vast cloud of dust mushroomed upward, gleaming with a myriad rainbow hues as the sunlight filtered through its interstices. It quickly cleared away in the strong up-draft and revealed chaos beneath.

The bowl was filled with broken stone that nearly flushed the lip of the slope. The cave mouth in the far cliff had vanished. Vanished too were the snakes and what was left of Crane Arnold.

Chapter Eighteen

Sick and dizzy, Slade sagged against the cliff wall. He tried to hold himself erect, but he was utterly spent and slid down it to a sitting position. Blood was streaming down his arm and his side felt as if every rib was smashed to splinters.

With trembling fingers he managed to tear open his shirt and after a brief examination thankfully decided that although the slug had hit him a terrific wallop, only the flesh was slashed open and so far as he could ascertain there were no broken bones.

Old Ben came tottering over to him. "Hold it, son, steady," he said. "I'm getting my strength back and I know how to handle hurts. Let me get your neckerchief off and I'll see what I can do to stop that blasted bleeding from your arm. The rip along your ribs hurts but it'll soon dry up by itself."

The gnarled old fingers worked deftly and soon the wounded arm was padded and bandaged and the blood flow had subsided to a trickle.

"Feeling better?" Sutler asked.

"Much," Slade replied. "I wonder if there's any water in this infernal hole?"

"There's some in the cave where they kept me chained up," Sutler replied. "I'll get it."

He shambled off to return a few minutes later with a bucket and a rusty tin cup. The water in the pail was cool and sweet and Slade absorbed about a pint of it. Then he managed to roll and light a cigarette.

"I've got a roll of bandage and some salve in my saddle pouch," he told Suffer. "I'll plaster up my side when we get out of this. How you feeling?"

"Pretty good now," old Ben declared with vigor. "I'm nigh onto starved and a bit weak but seeing those devils get what was coming to them was nigh as good as a big snort of likker would be. They trailed me here one night, caught me and kept me prisoner in one of the caves on this side. They made me go over and bring the gold from the cave on the other side of the pit. Nobody but me could cross over and not die of rattler poison, but I got a way with varmints. I was all right till I began to get too tired and weak. That made me nervous and I thought the trip I just made was my last. Reckon it would have been if it hadn't been for you, son. Ain't no use to try and thank you, but there's a purty sizeable pile of metal over there that you're welcome to as part pay."

Slade glanced curiously at the heaped blanket. "It was cached gold, wasn't it?" he asked.

Old Ben nodded vigorously. "Uh-huh, these cliffs are part of the *Sierra de Cenizas* — the Ashes Mountains — as the old Spaniard Captain de Gavilan called them. And over in that cave the other side of the snake pit is where de Gavilan hid his gold when the Pueblo uprising busted loose. There never was any argument but that de Gavilan and his bunch took a heck of a sight of gold out of his section of the Guadalupes. In the old missions down in Mexico there are writings that tell all about it. I saw 'em when I was a young feller and one of the old priests read 'em to me. It was him gave me the first notion about the gold hid here. He said that the uprising came mighty sudden and that de Gavilan and his men had been up here for months at the time. Wasn't hard to figure that they were digging out more gold and cacheing it somewhere. When the Pueblos went on the war-path they didn't have time to pack out with them what they'd dug. They brought some, but not much, so the old writings said. They sure must have skalleyhooted when they started. I found a regular trail of dropped nuggets through that crack in the cliffs."

Slade rolled old Ben a cigarette and listened with absorbing interest to this vivid account of hidden treasure and blood.

"I found a couple of skeletons near the mouth of the cleft, too," old Ben went on, "and some bits of rusted-away armor. I buried the skeletons, knowing those old fellers set a heap of store in having their bones put underground. Reckon the Indians did for them while they were trying to get away. Some did get away, including de Gavilan himself, of course, according to what the priest said, although most folks believe he was killed in the uprising. The old priest didn't know for sure whether de Gavilan ever told anybody he had gold hid here, but figured he must have mentioned it and planned to come back and get it. But de Gavilan and the few fellers who got out with him went back to Spain and died there, or so the priest said. The yarn sure did interest me and I started hunting for de Gavilan's gold. Sometimes I think I must have got a bit loco about it. Times when I nearly starved. Times when I passed over what looked to be good prospecting ground, especially in Jericho Valley. I'd have de Gavilan's gold or nothing. I hunted it for fifty years. And when I uncovered gold-bearing gravel at the bottom of the shale banks in Jericho Valley, I knew I was on the right track."

He paused, puffing hard on his cigarette, and laughed a little before he started talking again.

"Uh-huh, I found gold in paying quantities there in the valley, but I passed it up. I was too plumb excited to take any interest in it. The old writings said de Gavilan's gold was nuggets and wire gold, and that's what I'd uncovered in the valley. I'd already been over every foot of that hole, or so I thought, so I sat down by my campfire and started thinking, and the notion came to me that maybe the old Mexican had hid it somewhere in the cliffs up this way, though they sure didn't look promising. So I started going over the cliffs, foot by foot. Took me a long time to work up this far. Then all of a sudden I hit it, that crack in the cliffs that fellers riding the trail or even walking it would pass by a hundred times without seeing."

"And you followed the crevice," Slade prompted.

"That's right," said Sutler. "I came out of

the hole here and saw the snakes. Reckon they weren't here in de Gavilan's day. Never had seen so many snakes. But snakes don't faze me and I could see that hole in the wall across the pit. Right then, after finding the skeletons and the dropped nuggets in the crack, I knew that was it. So I crossed over without getting fanged and found it cached there in the cave, where a shaft leads up to the outer air. It had been put in buckskin sacks, but of course the sacks had long ago rotted away and it was all scattered about over the rock floor, heaps and heaps of it. I started bringing it out, and I reckon I was still a bit loco — maybe I still am — but I got an awful lot of fun out of bringing a few pokes at a time and teasing the boys. I figured I had a right to, after showing them the deposits in the valley. They just darn near went loco themselves and tried to follow me here and everything. But I'm pretty good at covering a trail and they didn't catch up with me till some hellions did a couple of months back. There were a couple of the bunch — they weren't here today — who were mighty good at trailing and brush work and they grabbed me."

He paused to glance apprehensively down the dark crevice. "Don't reckon they might show up, do you?" he asked.

"Don't worry," Slade told him. "They won't. They've been taken care of."

"Fine!" applauded old Ben. "I'm feeling better by the minute. Yes, they caught me, this side of the snake pit, and kept me chained up. They'd make me go over every now and then and bring back a load. Nobody but me could cross over and not die of rattler poison."

"Which was lucky for you," Slade interpolated. "Otherwise they'd have shot you without wasting any time."

"Guess that's right," agreed Sutler. "For a while, anyhow, I was worth more to 'em alive than dead. They'd feed me now and then and leave me a little grub, just enough to keep me strong enough to pack out the gold. Sometimes, like last night when Berry was here, they'd let me sleep over there in the cave, where it's warm."

Slade abruptly asked an indirect question. "When I was coming through the cleft and passed those last caves I thought I heard a horse blow back in one of them."

Old Ben chuckled. "That's my old skewbald," he said. "Funny thing about devils like that bunch — you never can figure what they'll do. They didn't kill the horse but looked after him and fed him better'n they did me. I brought him in with me always when I came here. A purty tight squeeze for him in some of the narrow places but he's lanky and made it. Hope he hasn't got too fat doing nothing to make it back to the outside."

"I've a notion we'll be able to shove him through," Slade smiled. "He'll come in handy to pack the gold to the outside. It would make a heavy load for two men who are hardly up to snuff."

"I'll get him," Sutler said. He shambled into the crevice and a few minutes later returned leading a salty looking cayuse who blinked dazzled eyes in the sunlight and regarded Slade dubiously.

However when El Halcon stretched out a fearless hand to him he did not object and seemed to enjoy having his nose rubbed.

"You got a way with critters, too," old Ben nodded. "Wouldn't be surprised if you could learn to handle snakes. I'll give you a few pointers if you like."

"No, thanks," Slade returned hastily. "After looking into that pit I never want to see another. Well, if you feel up to it, we might as well be moving. We've got a hard drag through that crack. Once we get outside I've some chuck in my saddle pouches and will be able to throw together a meal which we both can use. When we get to Sotol you can really line your belly again."

"And a great big snort of likker," old Ben added, smacking his lips with anticipation. "Let's get busy with that metal."

Sutler rooted out a couple more buckskin bags from the cave where he had been imprisoned and they sacked the gold and loaded it on the skewbald.

"A hefty heap and worth plenty," Slade remarked. "Also, I've a notion you won't have much trouble tieing onto most of what Arnold and Berry banked. Old-timer, you've had a tough experience, but now you're sitting pretty."

"Share and share alike," declared Ben. "You've sure earned yours."

Slade smiled and shook his head. "I've got a few pesos set aside against a rainy day," he explained. "A jigger in my line of work doesn't need much money — no time to spend it. Let's go, the new sheriff can come up and pack in the bodies if he's a mind to. Reckon he'll find he's got a considerable chore on his hands if he figures to root out Arnold's from under those rocks."

"Reckon he wouldn't be able to tell him from the rest of the snakes, the ornery varmint!" Sutler growled.

It was a hard drag through the cleft and they made slow progress. Sutler was still weak from hunger and Slade was far from being his normal self. At several of the narrow places they had to unload the horse to get him through. The sun was well down in the west when they at last stumbled wearily into the open air.

Slade's first chore was to care for the horses ridden by Arnold and Yates. Without much trouble he also located Berry's mount and provided for its wants.

"They can pack the gold to town," he told Sutler. "You can ride your critter."

As the sun was sinking behind the western crags, Slade made a fire and threw together an appetizing meal of bacon, eggs, coffee and dough cakes, of which both ate heartily, for they were famished. Then they built up the fire, stretched out beside it and slept till dawn.

Wishing to avoid the inevitable questioning and delay they would encounter if they passed the mining claims, Slade kept well to the west as they rode down the valley. Without meeting anybody they reached the Mojo Trail and headed for town. Old Ben had filled a small poke with nuggets. Now he drew it forth with a chuckle.

"Going to have one last little joke on the boys," he announced. "Let me do the talking first, son."

Upon reaching Sotol they stopped first at the livery stable to obtain quarters for the horses and to give the gold into the charge of the astounded Frank Nance. Then together they repaired to the Dun Cow.

Conversation in the saloon fell flat as Slade entered, the star of the Rangers gleaming on his breast, beside him old Ben who looked calmly about and headed straight for the bar. The goggle-eyed bartender stared at him, his mouth working but no words coming forth.

Old Ben up-ended his poke and nuggets rained on the bar. "Give us a drink!" he thundered. "Give everybody a drink!"

The bartender gasped, found his voice. "Ben!" he quavered. "Ben, is it really you and not a blasted ghost?"

"Whiskey!" roared Mr. Sutler, uncompromisingly.

Utter pandemonium broke loose, everybody shouting, yelling, howling questions. Old Ben gulped his drink, refilled his glass and ordered everything to eat the house could provide.

A little later, leaving Ben Sutler surrounded with food, drink and a crowd that hung on his every word as he told the story of his adventures and the part Slade played,

Slade slipped out and headed for the doctor's office. He felt a little medical attention was in order.

Doc Cooper stared at the Ranger star on Slade's breast, but he was a doctor first off and he asked no questions as he went to work on the patient.

"Nothing to it for a husky young feller like you," was his verdict after the chore was finished. "You'll be a mite stiff and sore for a few days but that should be all. Now would you mind telling me how you got those punctures, and a few other things, before I bust wide open with curiosity!"

That night there was a meeting of the commissioners and others in the sheriff's office. Tom Horrel was duly appointed sheriff to replace the dead Clifton Yates.

"Hope you manage to stay in one piece for a while, Tom," Wes Hargrove remarked. "We ain't been having much luck with sheriffs of late. The way those two hellions put it over on us is a caution to cats! I'd never have believed any skullduggery from Arnold and Yates. Russ Berry, yes, but not Arnold and Yates. Slade, you sure did a good chore and a smart one."

"They were smooth operators, all right," Slade agreed.

"But not quite smooth enough to buck El Halcon," observed old Sam Yelverton.

"To buck the Texas Rangers," Slade corrected smilingly. "But if I hadn't just happened to notice the resemblance between Arnold and Yates, the chances are they would have kept on putting it over," he added in deprecation of his own achievement.

"More'n anybody else noticed," said Yelverton. "But it's a pity you couldn't bring 'em in alive so we would have had the pleasure of hanging the varmints."

Slade smilingly shook his head. "I think it's best as it is," he said. "You might have had considerable difficulty hanging them if they'd stuck together and refused to talk. The only thing we would have had on them was that they robbed Ben Sutler. Chances are they've have just gotten prison sentences and after a while would have been turned loose to cause more trouble. As it is, I think they'll stay put. Well, everything worked out okay. The brains of the outfit is squashed, under a few tons of rock, and when you squash the head of that sort of a snake you don't have to worry much about the body. There may be a few minor characters still circulating around, who did chores for Arnold and Yates, but they're in the nature of hired hands and don't amount to much. If they stay in the section, which I figure is unlikely, the chances are Tom will round them up for some petty skullduggery, sooner or later. Now I think it would be a good idea for all of us to go over to the Dun Cow and give old Ben a hand in his celebration. Somebody'll have to put him to bed after a bit, judging from the way he was going this afternoon. And then I'm going to bed and nurse my scratches. Got to be riding tomorrow. Captain Jim will have something else lined up for me by the time I get back to the post. I'll tell him hello for you, Sam."

"Do that," said Yelverton, "and tell him from me he sure knows how to pick 'em!"

They watched him ride away the next morning, tall and graceful atop his great black horse, making light of his wounds and eager for the new adventure waiting over the next hilltop.

ABOUT THE AUTHOR

Bradford Scott was a pseudonym for Leslie Scott who was born in Lewisburg, West Virginia. During the Great War, he joined the French Foreign Legion and spent four years in the trenches. In the 1920s he worked as a mining engineer and bridge builder in the western American states and in China before settling in New York. A barroom discussion in 1934 with Leo Margulies, who was managing editor for Standard Magazines, prompted Scott to try writing fiction. He went on to create two of the most notable series characters in Western pulp magazines. In 1936, Standard Magazines launched, and in *Texas Rangers,* Scott under the house name of Jackson Cole created Jim Hatfield, Texas Ranger, a character whose popularity was so great with readers that this magazine featuring his adventures lasted until 1958. When others eventually began contributing Jim Hatfield stories,

Scott created another Texas Ranger hero, Walt Slade, better known as *El Halcon,* the Hawk, whose exploits were regularly featured in *Thrilling Western.* In the 1950s Scott moved quickly into writing book-length adventures about both Jim Hatfield and Walt Slade in long series of original paperback Westerns. At the same time, however, Scott was also doing some of his best work in hardcover Westerns published by Arcadia House; thoughtful, well-constructed stories, with engaging characters and authentic settings and situations. Among the best of these, surely, are *Silver City* (1953), *Longhorn Empire* (1954), *The Trail Builders* (1956), and *Blood on the Rio Grande* (1959). In these hardcover Westerns, many of which have never been reprinted, Scott proved himself highly capable of writing traditional Western stories with characters who have sufficient depth to change in the course of the narrative and with a degree of authenticity and historical accuracy absent from many of his series stories.

We hope you have enjoyed this Large Print book. Other Thorndike, Wheeler, and Chivers Press Large Print books are available at your library or directly from the publishers.

For information about current and upcoming titles, please call or write, without obligation, to:

Publisher
Thorndike Press
295 Kennedy Memorial Drive
Waterville, ME 04901
Tel. (800) 223-1244

or visit our Web site at:

http://gale.cengage.com/thorndike

OR

Chivers Large Print
published by BBC Audiobooks Ltd
St James House, The Square
Lower Bristol Road
Bath BA2 3SB
England
Tel. +44(0) 800 136919
email: bbcaudiobooks@bbc.co.uk
www.bbcaudiobooks.co.uk

All our Large Print titles are designed for easy reading, and all our books are made to last.